DROWNING IN HOT WATER

ISBN 1-892323-94-X
Library of Congress Card Number 00-103866
An original Publication of Vivisphere Publishing.
Printed in the U.S.A.

Vivisphere Publishing
a Division of NetPub Corporation
2 Neptune Road, Poughkeepsie, NY 12601

VIVISPHERE
PUBLISHING

www.vivisphere.com

For Eileen Murphy and Tom Sitter.

With thanks to my publisher, Peter Cooper, my editor, Fran Platt, and my agent, Paula Beck for their confidence in the book and their advice to me, and with gratitude for the encouragement and advice offered by Antoinette Tronco, Sherry Fox, John Friedman, Bill Martin, and Nancy Gargano, and as always, to Susan, Matt and Joe.

DROWNING IN HOT WATER

PATRICK T. MURPHY

VIVISPHERE
PUBLISHING

Chapter One

Lake Michigan's soft waves lap over the feet of what had been a young black male, now a bloated bluish corpse. Late-season swimmers and sunbathers form a semicircle around the body. Paramedics attend a bikinied 18-year-old, still hysterical because the body brushed against her leg on its way to the shore of the North Avenue Beach. A couple of wagon guys kneel, preparing a vinyl bag to transport the body to the Medical Examiner's office. A police photographer records the body and the scene. Doperton, my partner, haunches next to the body playing the role of a pensive detective for the benefit of the semicircle.

But there's really not much to do until the body is carted off and printed—when we just might discover that the pre-death young man was recently discharged from a state hospital. After a week homeless and without medication, he drifted back into psychosis, went up to the pier off Fullerton and dove into the lake, striking his head on a submerged rock. Or he could have been a druggie shooting up on the rocks off Fullerton, who got a little too juiced up, leaned over too far, fell, hit his head and drowned. Or just maybe he pushed the wrong guy's button the wrong way and got slapped upside the head with a baseball bat.

But there'll be time enough to figure that out. For now it's a beautiful day to stand on the beach at the edge of the lake. A few puffy white clouds drift under a bright blue sky. The temperature hovers in the high 70s, with Chicago's equatorial-like August humidity several weeks in the past. I look back at the bloated body and feel a tinge of guilt for enjoying a beautiful day at the shore. But then my pager interrupts. An unfamiliar number at first. Then it registers: Emily's school. I call back on my portable, reliving the morning's exchange:

"Mommy, I'm sick."

"Emily, darling, you've said that every day since you started first grade, and that's three weeks now."

"But this time it's true."

"And that's what you said yesterday."

"I was sick yesterday."

"And the day before?"

"I thought I was."

So I gave her a teaspoon of Children's Tylenol—more as a placebo, but nonetheless feeling guilty as I dragged her off to her first-grade classroom and Liam, my two-year-old, to Angela, our child care person.

"Carol Carper," the school secretary says—because my daughter's name is Carper, although the school records clearly show mine to be Moore. "Emily is complaining of a sore throat and headache."

"Does she have a fever?"

"No, but she appears to be a fairly sick young lady."

"I'll call right back."

"Will you be here soon? She's lying on a couch in the office. It's the only place, and I..."

"Yes, please; just a minute or two." Anger replaces angst. Why did the school secretary phone me, not Jeffrey, whose name appears first on the responsible relative list? But what school official will call Dad, even if Mom is standing on the Oak Street Beach investigating a death that may or may not be a homicide, while Dad sits staring dreamy-eyed out the window of his tiny office at Loyola University trying to figure out how to make English literature interesting to kids raised on MTV?

But guilt overwhelms anger. Is my career blinding me to my children's needs? And what is this career? A very tiny portion of the time fiction. But anger triumphs as I think of Jeffrey. I see into his mind: cluttered, brilliant but still relatively simple as he occasionally cooks, stacks dishes in the dishwasher, mops the floor and changes diapers, in between correcting papers and reading Graham Greene novels for the one-hundredth time, "getting new meaning" out of each paragraph. A modern man. A partner. A companion. Even a feminist, of sorts; or so he thinks. But while he

8

read and reread and reread again the same Greene books preparing his dissertation, I nursed and cared for Emily, worked a squad in a district regarded as "quiet" if we only had a dozen shootings on a summer weekend, and too often fended off partners inadvertently rubbing against my butt or breasts.

Jeffrey's long-winded voicemail informs me that he's occupied. Just leave a message—unless I'm a student in need of his assistance, in which case I'm told to show up at a certain hour; but if I'm a graduate student I should press another number to record a different message. But since I'm just his wife with an emergency involving his daughter, I can leave a message or press zero and reach a human being. I hit the zero and get his voicemail again. I'm about to throw the phone into the lake when my partner, Cy Doperton, observes, "That fella had one ugly gash on his head."

"It's in my report," I say.

"Good. Who you talking to?"

"Business. Old Vice stuff."

I don't need Doperton knowing my business. I walk away from him and phone the general number and ultimately get the English Department secretary, who informs me that "Dr. Carper is with a graduate student. Shall I interrupt?"

My sanity, and certainly Emily's health—presuming she is really ill—are more important than the gorgeous 23-year-old with horn-rimmed glasses, long blonde hair and a miniskirt exposing long, tan, athletic legs I imagine sitting across from Jeffrey, cooing at his pearls of wisdom. I cajole the secretary into getting Jeffrey on the phone. He is accommodating. "Of course; poor dear. I would rather not cancel my classes this afternoon. If she's not too bad, do you think it will be all right if I dropped her at Angela's? I'll come right back after class and get her by four o'clock."

Accommodation. Many women, most women, would love that in a companion. But only Jeffrey can take a decent trait and use it—quite unconsciously, I presume—to drive me crazy.

Accommodation. No fighting. But no real discourse. In 12 years of marriage, we've never argued; but neither have we talked, really talked. Concerns, problems, disagreements that arise when two people share close quarters, children and their bodies get shoved aside and ultimately ignored by "Let's not quibble over irrelevancies," or "Our relationship is too important to sweat the small stuff," or "Honey, I love you." *The End of the Affair* or *A Burnt-out Case* excites Jeffrey much more than my body. I'm amazed on one hand, but irritated on the other, that most men seem to covet what Jeffrey takes for granted or out of duty.

"That body bother you?" Doperton says as we pull away.

"I've been on the force 12 years."

"But Homicide less than a year."

"People prematurely dead bother me."

"Go back to Vice."

"I dislike bodies, not Homicide. Vice I disliked."

"You were a decoy whore in Vice?"

"On occasion."

He leans over and his eyes scope me like a modeling agent who still appreciates his clientele. I wait for him to tick off my tiresome attributes: 5' 7", dark blonde hair, hazel eyes, clear skin, long legs, maybe 130 pounds. Instead he shakes his head and says, "Shit, you probably had to ugly up to make any kind of real decoy."

I look out the window at the skyline. The type of man I dealt with as a decoy prostitute would come on to his grandmother if she were wearing a short skirt, spike heels, a garter belt and a black or red pointy bra.

"Incidentally, kid, I'm gonna get sick for a couple of weeks, so you'll go this one alone."

"You're ill?" I ask, knowing he's disgustingly healthy for someone about to retire.

He laughs. "Got all those sick days. I'd feel cheated if I had to give them back to the city."

"An M.D. will back you up?"

"My wife's cousin's husband is a foot doctor. And this case should be a no-brainer."

Back at the office, I input my report into the computer and phone Jeffrey. "Emily's fine. Her stomachache and sore throat didn't much bother her as she wolfed down an ice cream cone. She was content to stay with Angela. I fear that our daughter has a slight case of first-grade blues."

I feel relieved that Emily is not sick, but guilty because I am not available, at least now, to help her through her anxiety. "I'll probably be a little late tonight."

"What's up?"

"A homicide."

"Jeez."

"Homicide is the safest division on the force. Our clients are already dead."

"Someone's killed them."

"And I'm also wearing a 9-millimeter. Besides, I'd never be so stupid as to go into a dangerous place without backup."

So we prattle on, dealing with housekeeping matters. Jeff will provide macaroni and cheese for the children. I'll do some light shopping on the way home. He'll give them their baths and I'll get them to bed. And what about the canceled check? The phone bill? MasterCard?

Jeff and I run a business. We care for Liam and Emily, buy groceries, pay the mortgage, make car payments, balance our schedules to meet these needs. Occasionally we get a babysitter and go out to dinner, but before long we're into corporate matters— which is okay. But this isn't the wild, uninhibited romance that I thought I had signed on for.

I was a 22-year-old drama student when I met Jeffrey, a graduate student. He quoted Wilde with apparent familiarity and was the only human I had ever met who seemed to understand *Finnegan's Wake*. More importantly, he was an expert on Beckett. Over the next two years, my love for the theater diminished as my love for Jeffrey increased. My incipient career ultimately foundered on the shoals of a nasty review. I had played a cop at a small neighborhood theater. The reviewer disliked the play, but also went out of his way to single me out: I was "too pretty" for the role; but more than that, I played it with too much sophistication and culture for a police officer.

The review appeared in a nothing community newspaper and was probably read by only a few people, but to me it might as well have been the *New York Times*. I was devastated. But I was also pissed. I would show the reviewer: I decided to study for and take the police exam. I came in second. A new career was born. In the theater, I'd be just one more ingenue pretending to be someone else. As I studied for the police exam, I decided that I wanted to *be* that someone else.

While our early years were not exactly out of *La Boheme* we lived in a one-bedroom flat and scrimped and saved our way through Jeff's Ph.D. But we had fun. Emily came as Jeff was preparing to defend his dissertation. Now, my women friends rave about Jeff and how lucky I am to have a husband who cooks, occasionally does the dishes and even vacuums. No one praises *me* for doing all of that—and a lot more, most of the time—and all of it until I went on the Vice Squad. I'm not complaining. I love even the worst aspects of childrearing, like rocking a wailing child at three in the morning and trying to prevent myself from falling asleep and dropping the baby on her head.

Shortly before Liam was born, I began doubting our relationship. I pushed my concerns aside, but with increasing frequency they reappeared. Now when Jeff and I are alone, I often feel smothered. But when I see Liam or Emily or go for a walk with them and Jeffrey, I feel okay again, and guilty about my anxiety. And then Jeffrey and I spend time together alone, or make love, and I want to scream.

And then there's Andrew. Andrew I met shortly after being assigned to Homicide. My former chief, the head of Vice, asked me to help in a sting operation. In the previous month, three attractive professional women in their thirties had been attacked. In each case, the women in Chicago on business had stopped for a cup of coffee or a drink at a hotel bar or restaurant. A man apparently followed them off the elevator, walked up behind them, put a half-Nelson around their neck, reached under their skirt, grabbed their crotch and beat it out the nearest staircase. The women in question wore glasses—which he knocked off—and wore short skirts. The attacks occurred in three different very posh hotels. The damage was minimal, and the hotels, the city and the media more or less conspired not to publicize the assaults and cause a hemorrhage of convention business.

So I made the round of upscale hotel bars, where I sat alone, read a magazine, had a glass of wine and then went to an upper floor, where my backups waited in stairwells and hotel rooms. It was pretty boring stuff, as much police work is. But at least I got to put the kids to bed, since we didn't start our rounds until about eleven.

After two weeks, nothing happened - though one more young professional woman was attacked, resulting in a small article in the back of the paper: *"Woman knocked unconscious in hotel."* The article implied that the police were investigating a possible domestic squabble. But even this lie was enough to send tremors throughout the city's business and political establishments that rumbled their way to the Police Commissioner, then to a captain and ultimately to the chief of Vice—which of course led to my backups and me. "What the fuck are you people doing? And you," he shouted, shaking a finger at me, "you look like a fucking schoolteacher."

"Chief, this is not about prostitutes. He's grabbing professional women."

"Well, wear something to stand out from the crowd. This guy is obviously interested in buns, so flaunt them."

Of course the chief was wrong. If the guy were really interested in someone's rear end, he'd go to a local whore bar. This guy simply wanted to diss professional women. And when he was apprehended several weeks later (without my help), that turned out to be the case. We didn't collar him. He assaulted a professionally attired 40-year-old. The element of surprise didn't work. She struggled, screamed, kneed him and chased him into the stairwell. By the time he got to the first floor, the entire security staff was waiting for him.

The next weekend, I wore a sleeveless, almost-sheer blouse and a brief skirt that, from the right angle, exposed my underwear. I was eyed by every guy at the bar and approached by three, whom I politely put off. When I left, a portly fellow in his mid-60s stumbled after me onto the otherwise-empty elevator. As the doors closed, he sloshed, "Would you be insulted if I informed you that you have a succulent bottom?"

13

"No more than if my father had."

"But I'm not your father," he said, straightening his tie and slicking back his graying dark hair, "and I'm a hell of a lot richer."

I didn't say anything. I got off the elevator. So did he. I walked fast, but he fell in behind. "I got a right to be here, you know."

I didn't reply, but picked up my pace, hoping that my backups were ready. Suddenly two large paws engulfed my breasts from behind. Instinctively I screamed. Doors opened and three of Chicago's Finest descended on my attacker, throwing him against the wall. The largest, youngest and least experienced (who also had a thing for me) shouted, "Attack my partner, you sick son-of-a-bitch?" and pounded the old fellow in the stomach. The others grabbed at him. I leapt in front of the aggressor-turned-victim, who turned ashen and then retched all over my sleeveless blouse and skirt. He sagged to the floor grasping his chest.

"Christ, the son-of-a-bitch got a heart attack! Give him CPR," one of the guys yelled, "and phone for the paramedics!" We looked at the guy on the floor, his face covered with vomit. None of us ventured to give CPR.

In any event, he was breathing, hadn't had a heart attack, was not our crotch-grabbing bandit but was one very drunk, very rich CEO of a major corporation with tons of resources—meaning money, and thus an equivalent amount of clout. My arrest of the CEO on misdemeanor sexual assault charges sent tremors through the local business and political establishments that rumbled through to the commander, the captains, the chief and ultimately to us. "Why the fuck did you slug the son-of-a-bitch?" he screamed.

"He attacked a police officer, my partner," the defender of my virtue argued.

"It's not as if she was in uniform. She was dressed like a fuckin' hooker."

I bit my tongue to keep from giving the chief a tongue-lashing, instead saying, "There was no offer of money for sex. Besides, I wasn't dressed like a hooker. I was dressed like a businessperson. And it was an assault.'

"Then you should have cuffed him."

"It was self-defense," the detective lied.

14

"He was a 64-year-old drunk. He claims he was minding his own business when he was viciously assaulted. And he's also worth a hundred times our combined annual incomes. The judge obviously didn't think much of our charges, since she let him out on his own recognizance."

News of the arrest of the CEO of a *Fortune* 500 company couldn't be suppressed; but it didn't make a big splash either, since all parties went out of their way to downplay the incident—which gave everyone plenty of maneuvering room. City Hall expressed complete confidence in its police department, but reserved judgment on the incident until the courts heard the evidence. The corporation spun the event by claiming that the CEO was taking an unnamed prescription drug for an unnamed ailment, had had a glass of wine, which caused him to become disoriented and pass out. He had no recollection of the events. The Chicago Police Department stated that the CEO was charged with a misdemeanor—inappropriate touching—but recognized that he was disoriented when arrested.

The case was heard in a municipal courtroom on the top floor of the main police building, where new or cloutless judges preside over grimy courtrooms filled with prostitutes, jackrollers, adolescents who steal ten-year-old cars and homeless should-be mental patients who defecate on State Street. Most are represented by young, inexperienced Public Defenders who object to every question put by young, inexperienced State's Attorneys:

"What did you see him doing?"

"Objection."

"Reason?"

"Irrelevant."

"Overruled."

One or two defendants are represented by private counsel, fast-talking out of the sides of their mouths, who generally know even less than the Public Defenders. Nevertheless, most judges treat them like geniuses.

Once in a while a defendant with resources gets dragged into the Municipal Court net. On that rare occasion a real lawyer appears, causing most judges to roll out the red carpet—which is precisely what occurred when Andrew Malcolm strolled into the courtroom.

15

Malcolm is a partner at *the* firm in Chicago. He does it all—criminal, civil, trials and appeals—wins most, and charges the highest fees in the city. When I first saw him in court that day, I couldn't vouch for his brilliance, but I could for his sex appeal. He was – is—easily the most striking example of male good looks that I've seen outside of a movie screen: early forties, maybe 6' 2", clear, unblemished, medium complexion, high-cheekboned face, slate-blue eyes, auburn hair and probably 190 pounds of what I fantasize to be a firm but not overly muscular body. Handsome but not too.

The judge, a blushing fifty-something woman, had the case called first. Four of us spread out behind the Assistant State's Attorney. Malcolm stood by himself. Unlike the typical Municipal Court attorney who believes that volume equals knowledge, Malcolm spoke softly. Unlike the PDs who ramble on valiantly but hopelessly trying to make a silk purse out of a sow's ear, Malcolm, both before the bench and later in chambers, was low-key and to the point. And unlike the State's Attorneys who think that arrogance and preening pass for intelligence, Malcolm was modest, even deferential. "Your Honor, my name is Andrew Malcolm, and I represent the defendant in this case. I suggest that it could assist all the parties and the court if we were to confer in chambers to discuss the facts and implications of this case."

"Mr. Malcolm might be a hotshot civil lawyer, but he apparently doesn't know the first rule of criminal procedure. The defendant must be in court unless his presence is specifically waived by the judge. Further, Your Honor, the defendant has an absolute right to be present at any in-chambers conference, and only he can waive his right to be absent. To do otherwise is reversible error. Since he's not here, I ask that you revoke his bond and issue an arrest warrant." The Assistant State's Attorney stood on his toes, strutted a bit and peered over his shoulder at the reporters sitting in the first row.

The threat of instantaneous incarceration for his client didn't faze Malcolm. "Of course the defendant must be present, and he's in the building. I can produce him in minutes. Because I do not wish to turn his proceeding into a circus, I have asked him to stay away for the time being. As an officer of the court, I am informing Your Honor that my client agrees with the in-chambers conference. He will appear when you wish."

"I object," the State's Attorney said, cutting Malcolm off. "I will not attend. Number one, only the defendant can agree to such a meeting. Number two, only the state, under the separation of powers doctrine, has the power to charge or dismiss a case; so there can be no conference unless we attend."

"Your Honor…" Malcolm began, but the judge cut him off.

"Just a second, Mr. Malcolm." She turned to the Assistant State's Attorney: "Mr. Malcolm is an attorney with a track record. If he tells me that his client wants a conference, I believe him and will hear him out. And you are quite right that only the state can prosecute and dismiss under the separation of powers doctrine; but under that same doctrine, only the court or jury can judge and sentence. Is this a bench or jury trial, Mr. Malcolm?"

"A bench," Malcolm replied quickly. Even a fool would know which way the wind was blowing. Malcolm is anything but that. On the other hand, the State's Attorney…or perhaps he was calling the judge's bluff. "I won't attend the conference."

"I cannot conference a case unless all parties attend; but I can order the parties to confer, without the court's presence, about the guidelines with respect to pre-trial publicity and other matters, including possible settlement. Please do so now."

"Judge, I will only attend if Detective Moore is present," the assistant snarled. Lawyers frequently meet in person or over the phone to discuss cases. But on occasion, particularly in the past in misdemeanor courts, where kinky municipal court lawyers at times tossed hundred-dollar bills at young prosecutors, a conscientious assistant would insist that a "prover", usually a cop, be present during discussions. So the assistant was insulting Malcolm.

Before the judge could launch into a tirade, Malcolm spoke: "Of course. We're here to cooperate."

"That's very gracious of you, Mr. Malcolm," she said.

We walked past the bench to the State's Attorney's office in the rear of the courtroom. The assistant opened the door and stormed in. Malcolm stepped aside and followed me. The three of us filled the tiny cluttered room. "So whaddaya want?" the young man asked, casually and without the rancor that courtrooms encourage.

"To resolve the matter amicably."

"And how do we do that when one of Chicago's Finest got pawed by your oafish client?"

"My client did in fact unjustifiably touch Detective Moore. But he was reacting to medication and out of his mind. He also is 64 years old, has never been arrested, served his nation both in the armed forces and as a consultant to Democratic and Republican presidents. The beating that he received in police custody could very well result in a seven-figure judgment against the city."

"And I suppose he has no memory of getting on the elevator with Detective Moore, remarking about her rear end and grabbing her breasts?"

"That's correct."

"Then how does he remember being beat up after his arrest?"

"I do not intend to argue my case. I felt that settlement discussions would limit the potential damage to everyone: your office, my client, the taxpayers. After my conversation with the first assistant yesterday, I thought that your office was interested in such a discourse."

The assistant unsuccessfully tried to conceal his anxiety. "I don't want to be too hasty. Go back to the courtroom and I'll be right there."

To make a brief story briefer, the assistant came back looking like he had been to the woodshed. We trooped into the judge's chambers and the deal was cut. Both sides agreed to execute mutual releases. Charges were dropped against Mr. CEO. He wrote me apologizing for any anguish that I'd suffered because he'd had a couple of glasses of wine (more like a gallon of Jack Daniels, I'd say) while taking undisclosed medication. As a result, he'd stumbled and thrust about for something to grab hold of—which turned out to be my breasts. Of course he didn't say exactly that; but stripped of its obfuscation, that's what the message was.

My comrades were irate. Not me: I don't take this stuff, at least the kind of stuff that happened in the hotel, seriously. So an old horny drunk grabbed me. In the hierarchy of offenses that I've seen, this is pretty minimal.

While in the judge's chambers, Andrew Malcolm eyed me the way subtle men do women whom they would like to know better. I wasn't surprised when a week later he phoned.

"Detective Moore?"

"Yes?"

"Andrew Malcolm."

After a hesitation, "Yes?"

"Do you have a minute?"

I answered, sounding slightly puzzled, "Well, yes."

He proceeded cautiously. "When a lawyer does a job for a client, he doesn't have to like the client. I detested what my client did."

"I know that, Mr. Malcolm."

"Andrew, please."

"I know that, Andrew, and please don't apologize. My job isn't to entice and arrest dirty old men. Frankly, I feel sorry for him."

"I don't…but that's another story, which we should discuss over a drink or dinner sometime."

"Is that an invitation?"

"Do you consider it one?"

"I'm a happily married, old-fashioned mother of two children."

"I'm also happily married, with three children. But I'm intrigued by what you do, and in you as a person—not as a..."

"Sex object? Too bad."

A pause. A giggle. "Tomorrow?"

I placed the phone down feeling giddy. Then guilty. From the moment I first laid eyes on Jeffrey, I had not lunched or dined with another man. I don't count the sandwiches and coffee shared with other cops. That was at worst work and at best camaraderie. But my first lunch with Andrew was precedent-setting.

The following day, as I approached the restaurant, feelings of disloyalty nibbled at my soul. I thought of turning and fleeing. But I wasn't about to have an affair. I was about to have a little bit of a life that wasn't the family of Jeffrey and Carol or the family of the CPD and Carol. And by so doing I even might make those two family lives a bit more exciting.

Our lunch ended up being as fun as it was innocent.
"What happened today in the world of the anti-crime establishment?" Andrew said, ignoring the menu.

"Not much. Blue-collar crime is pretty much an evening, nighttime affair."

"Yeah, it's the white-collar stuff, the kind I end up defending, that's daytime. And more insidious."

"Depends on your meaning of insidious. What I see is more violent, particularly toward the individual. White-collar crime probably hurts a few more people financially. Besides, the people who get ripped off for the most part can afford it."

Andrew hunched over, boring into me with his slate-blues: "Just what I expected."

"Huh?"

"You. You're not a cop. I mean you're not just a cop. You're a philosopher. College?"

"Northwestern."

"Not too many cops from Northwestern."

"I went there on a drama scholarship."

"That's quite a jump, from the theater to the police department. You have an actress' looks. With a scholarship, you must have had the ability. What happened?"

"Ingenues are a dime a dozen."

"But you were more than just an ingenue."

"I thought so. But the theater is a tough business: too much talent, too few opportunities. It can be depressing—even humiliating. It's so much a matter of luck, timing, connections and who you bed down. Besides, the type of drama that attracted me had even fewer opportunities and paid little." I smile as I recall those heady days. "I eschewed anything lighter than Beckett."

"Then you're back in your element?"

"How so?"

"Crime, criminals, Chicago Police Department."

"Yeah, the theater of the absurd."

"Have you done anything since college?"

"Not really. I loved acting, but I don't regret giving up on it. The intermittent burst of adrenaline that one gets as a cop is a lot

20

more regular and almost as high as one gets on the stage. Besides, the drama students I hung out with were not exactly *The Sound of Music* material. None of them made it, except for my roommate. For about a decade, she played in tiny theater productions while waitressing to make ends meet."

"So what's she doing now?"

"She married a wealthy businessman, lives in the furthest North Shore suburb possible and occasionally does the dinner theater stuff. Last year I saw her in *Cabaret*."

The waiter interrupted and we ordered. "So what do you like best about your job?"

"Apprehending the scum and getting convictions on them."

"And worst?"

"Apprehending the scum and getting convictions on them."

"And of course you'll explain this apparent contradiction."

"We arrest scum who prey on the weak. Our job is to get them off the street. But most of them wouldn't be scum if they weren't born at the wrong place, wrong time to the wrong people."

"A liberal cop."

"I'm neither liberal nor conservative. I'd like to think that I'm realistic."

"But philosophical, Detective Moore."

"Please...Carol."

"Then, Carol, does the end of collaring the scum justify cutting corners—constitutional and legal corners—here and there?"

"I can only speak for myself. I try to perform my duties as conscientiously and as ethically as I can."

"You still haven't answered the question."

"One can be philosophical when one has the luxury of time. In police work, critical events explode. You walk into a bar: Razors flash, guns come out. You bust into an apartment to arrest a seller: You don't know if you're going to get a blast in the face—if you'll see your kids again. Ends and means are irrelevant under those circumstances. It's not like being a lawyer. And, Andrew...Do lawyers consider whether the end justifies the means?"

"That's a topic we'll discuss on another occasion."

The hour was soon over. We parted with a handshake, and no suggestion of meeting again. But we both knew that we would. Two weeks later, we did, and practically every week since. Though our conversations had never become intimate, I assumed that at some point he'd hit on me, and that I would rebuff him. That would be the end of a friendship that I relish and lunches that I look forward to from the moment I depart the previous one.

But other than a handshake, he never touched me. Then about a month ago, while we were waiting for our cars, he placed his hand softly on the nape of my neck. I got into my car and drove away, but then pulled over. I trembled with excitement and curiosity. Then desire. Finally shame. I had betrayed Jeff. Lunches, calls and candid conversations had given Andrew the correct impression that he had permission to touch me. I hadn't committed adultery, but I felt shabby.

For a week I didn't return his calls; and then, when I did, I begged off seeing him for two additional weeks. On the last occasion he interrupted: "Carol."

"I'm so sorry, work..."

"Please...I get the feeling that you think I'm out to seduce you."

"Andrew, no, I'm sorry. I'm busy." But even as I mouth the words, I want to be seduced.

"Carol, hear me out. I like you as a person. I think of you as a dear friend—not as someone I want to bed down, but as a fellow human being, and one that I've never felt so...so much in common with..."

"Tomorrow."

And so we met in an hour filled with silence, half-hearted forking the food and a few desultory and feeble attempts to fill the void with insipid conversation. "How's your job?"

"How's your family?"

"How are the depositions in the Smith case?"

And, "Fine."

"Fine."

"Fine."

It wasn't because we had nothing to say that we didn't say much. Rather, each of us feared what we might say and then regret it. As we waited for the cars, he turned and faced me. I knew that he wanted to kiss me. Then, instantaneously, a look of confusion and terror moved across his face. My car arrived. "Until next week," he said and grasped my hand.

That was a week ago; and today I'm to see Andrew again. And I'm both relieved and upset that I have a legitimate excuse to avoid him. Can we go on like this much longer before the tension snaps and we do something that we both—at least I—will regret? That tension is terrible but exciting, stimulating, human. Long ago it vanished from my relationship with Jeffrey.

Often, when everyone is asleep, I stare outside the window into the night, thinking that my life—not Jeffrey—stifles me. When I was a young would-be actress, I devoured poetry. For the sake of just a poem, Rainer Rilke wrote, "You must see many cities, many people and things, you must understand animals, must feel how birds fly, and know the gesture which small flowers make when they open in the morning. You must be able to think back to streets and unknown neighborhoods, to unexpected encounters, and to partings you had long seen coming; to days of childhood whose mystery is still unexplained...You must have memory of many nights of love, each one different from all the others...Only then can it happen that in some very rare hour the first word of a poem arises in their midst and goes forth from them."

And where is the poetry in my life? Emily and Liam certainly. But is that it? And what happens when they no longer need me? What about romance? Sex? Love? A touch? What about the life buried in my psyche?

Is Jeffrey incapable of evoking the poetry buried in my soul? Do I delude myself to romanticize that Andrew will unshutter my psyche?

I phone Andrew to cancel our lunch. "Of course; work comes first. But what about later? Tonight?"

"I'll be at this pretty late. My daughter isn't feeling well."

"A quick cup of coffee. I...I'd like to see you."

I tell him that I might call later, and worry about why he needs to see me, particularly in the evening. Is he falling in love with me? And then it hits me: It's now more than romantic lunches and fantasies of seduction. I am falling in love with him. I bury the thought and get back to the young man on the beach.

CHAPTER 2

In life the corpse had been Howard Pore, age 34. He spent half of the last half of his life behind bars: aggravated battery, possession of heroin, burglary and a half a dozen dismissals. Over the past two years, burnout had settled in. No jail time. Several arrests for public intoxication and possession.

I ask Doperton if he wants to go out to Howard's last known address, with predictable results. I drive out to the West Side and pull up in front of a crumbling three-story brick affair that hasn't seen a tuckpointer since before Pearl Harbor. A couple of teens swagger by. One yells, "Hey, you gotta fine honky ass, Ms. Social Worker." At least he doesn't fall down and grab my breasts for support.

The small entrance has three metal mailboxes, with a J. Pore over the third one. I unfasten the holster clip and clasp the 9mm and trudge to the third floor. A short, medium-built mid-forties woman opens the door. I flash my badge. "I'm trying to get some information on Howard Pore."

She doesn't look at my credentials. "He not be living here."

"Your name?"

"Jeanette Pore. I'm his Mom."

"No one has contacted you?"

"I ain't been seeing him but once in the last month. He been living here and there. But you looking for the wrong man. Howard ain't into trouble no more, 'cept for the drinkin'. He's straightened himself out."

The Medical Examiner's office apparently hadn't moved as quickly as I anticipated. My first instinct is to get out. Let someone else be the bad guy. But then she might not be so ready to deal with me afterwards. "May I come in?"

"Please."

A younger, heavyset woman lounges on a Salvation Army couch. Two kids about my own children's ages and a third in between tumble about the floor and race around the flat. Jeanette Pore stands before me looking like she expects the worst. She also looks like she's used to hearing the worst.

I tell her. She screams, runs into the bathroom and retches. The heavyset woman leaps up, bellows, "Mama!" and runs after her. The three kids wail and run after their mother and grandmother.

I remain alone. Helpless. Stupid. But remain. They are the widgets that I need to complete my work and justify my existence. After several minutes, Jeanette Pore emerges, her eyes red and swollen. "That honky whore bitch did it. She and her white-trash honky pervert boyfriend."

I put my arm around her. Her daughter does the same from the other direction and we sit on the couch. "Ms. Pore, we don't know how your son died yet."

"Howard didn't go swimming with his clothes on."

"He could have been walking on the rocks and fallen in."

"The honky bitch. She did it. She's a rotten bitch."

"Where will I find her?"

"The fuckin' bitch. She killed their baby, my beautiful grandchild. Now she's done in my son. My beautiful boy. May she burn in Hell. Dear Lord, forgive me, but avenge my poor, poor Howard. He was such good boy. Not always great, but he had a good, dear heart. He loved his baby. He loved his Mama."

"How can I find her?"

Mrs. Pore leaps up and flees back into the bedroom. I look at the daughter. She puts her head down and then looks at me shyly. "Forgive Mama. She doesn't mean no harm."

"What do you mean?"

"That honky white trash business."

"I've heard worse."

"My brother was common-law with this woman. Mama didn't approve."

"And you?"

"Howard's business. But I didn't take to her none. She's a lowlife doper."

"What about the child?"

"She and Howard had two girls. The two-year-old died but two months ago. Her biker boyfriend killed her, and the bitch did nothing. But neither been charged. Just one more nigger that's died. Who cares?"

"How'd it happen?"

"Scalded. Lilly—that's Howard's wife—said that the baby pulled a pot of water on top of her. I say he poured it on the baby. So did Howard. He was real upset. Went to the cops. 'Course they got rid of his black ass quick. Called the newspapers. They paid him no attention."

I inquire about Lilly's relationship with Howard and the biker.

"Howard and her took up together about eight, nine years ago, right before he went to Stateville the second time. They split for good about the time Precious was born. She was the baby that died. She met the biker buyin' drugs, I'm told. The live girl, Asha, she's about five. Lilly Higgins, that's the bitch. Don't know the boyfriend's name. Howard living no place in particular. Sometimes here. Sometimes on the street. Sometimes with friends. He's been actin' funny the last year or so."

A child pulling boiling water down onto herself seems more plausible than the Pore family version, but I've been in law enforcement too long to dismiss any hypothesis. I call the Medical Examiner's office and discover that a Precious Pore was killed seven weeks earlier. I get an address on Argyle. It's already dark when I pull up in front of an apartment building on the North Side in Uptown, not too different from the one that I just left on the West Side.

My pager goes off. It's Jeffrey. "Everything okay?"

"I'll be working late. My so-called partner wimped out on me."

"Where are you?"

"In Uptown on Argyle."

"Christ! That's a dangerous area."

"I have a gun."

27

"You're without a backup. What if some drug-crazed moron shoots you in the back? Remember the guy in the hotel?"

"For Christ's sake, Jeffrey. He grabbed my boobs"—with, I think angrily, more feeling than you've done in years.

"Next time it could be a razor."

"What a lovely thought. But you'll get a great pension if I'm killed in the line of duty."

"Don't be like that."

"I'm joking. How's Emily?"

"She's had two slices of pizza and a bowl of ice cream."

"Real healthy, Jeffrey. Veggies?"

"It's just one night."

"And Liam?"

"He's got diarrhea. Other than that he's a happy camper watching an old tape of *Sesame Street*."

"And Emily?"

"She's with him."

"No homework?"

"She's in her first month of first grade."

The pager beeps again. It's Andrew. "Got to go."

"Who's paging you?"

"Headquarters. Don't wait up. I could be late."

"Be careful."

"I'm getting lonely," Andrew says when I call.

"I don't know about this evening. I'll be late."

"I'll wait."

"I have to interview some folks. It might not be too long. I'll call."

"Where are you?"

"Up on Argyle in Uptown."

"By yourself?"

"Yes."

"Are you crazy?"

"I'm perfectly safe."

"I'll come meet you."

"Andrew, you're a lawyer, not a karate champ."

"I've got a suede belt in karate."

"Yeah. Wear it tonight. Call you soon."

Lilly Higgins is not out of central casting. I half-expect an overweight woman with massive breasts and behind sagging and surging out of a size-ten slip, peroxide hair on black roots, a lipstick-smeared cigarette in hand, a dozen empties lying around the floor. But the Lilly Higgins who opens the door is ice. She's about my height; her naturally medium blonde, wavy hair is a shade or two lighter than my own, and like mine falls just past her shoulders; her hazel eyes are a shade or two darker than my own. And from her build, I would think that she should weigh about the 128 that I do, but she leans more toward 120. She's dressed like she's not expecting company, at least the female kind. Two garments cover her body: a large, white, man's tee-shirt slithering just past her butt, and flimsy bikini underpants that are exposed when she crosses her legs. We sit in a neat, long room, furnished with a cheap couch, two matching chairs, a coffee table and the largest stereo system that I've seen outside of a nightclub.

"Too bad. Howard wasn't a bad guy—when he wasn't drinking, doping, screwing around and beating me and the kids. Of course I can't remember when he wasn't doing one or the other of those things."

"You were head over heels."

"Yeah, and stupid; and once in a while, when he was sober enough or not in the can, in love with the sex. Love: You tell me what it is. I'm too busy just tryin' to get by."

"No ideas on who would have murdered Howard?"

"Thought he might of drowned, accidental-like."

"Might have. Might not have."

"Not a lot of people liked Howard. Could be some wino buddy, or maybe one of the dozen or so folks he owed for drugs, or some guy he wronged in the joint."

"Or maybe your boyfriend."

"Sam ain't got nothin' to be jealous about, particularly from Howard. I wouldn't mess with Howard if he were...Shit. Why talk about it? He's dead. Not in a position to help me. Or shit on me."

"Is that what a relationship is?"

"Whaddaya mean?"

"Helping or hurting?"

29

"Are you a cop or psychiatrist?"

"I'm investigating a murder."

"Then why get into my social life?"

"Could be related to the homicide in question."

"So I hit Howard up top the head, dragged him to the North Avenue Beach and dumped his body..."

"Or had it done. Maybe you whispered sweet nothings into Sam's ear until he did it."

"Sam isn't a sweet-nothings type of guy. He's pretty much— what do you say?—an oaf."

"Like a lot of men."

Lilly smiles without mirth. "Just about all the guys I've known been like that, usually with pretty rotten results. But Sam's okay by me. Sometimes he even makes me feel okay."

"You ever work?"

"Whaddaya mean?"

"You know what I mean."

"Yeah, I was a working girl, when I was a kid. Got some arrests. Maybe convictions. Dunno."

"Recently?"

She stands abruptly and in a single motion pulls her tee-shirt off. "Whaddaya think?"

"Of what?"

"My body."

"Mine's better."

She bends over to pick up her tee-shirt, pumping her butt slowly while she does so. She slips it on and sits. "My body may leave you cold, but it drives all guys and more than a few women wild. But why give it away? Yeah. I charge if someone who don't turn me off wants a piece of me. Why not? It supplements the nickels and dimes I get from the lousy welfare check. But that doesn't make me a working girl. Check my rap sheet. I haven't been arrested in five, six years. I sell it only to my friends, or guys I trust. I'm no hooker. If a guy, or lady for that matter, wants to bed me down, they pay. It's business. I got something they want; so why shouldn't I make a few dollars off that?"

"Pretty romantic."

"And I'm different than your average professional chick who beds down with some asshole 'cause he buys her dinner? The folks I do aren't that hip. It's just, 'Hey, baby, how 'bout getting' it on?' or 'Lilly, I just love your big, firm tits; can we cuddle?' 'Sure, that'll be…' I say, and give them a price a few bucks more than they can afford. We bargain, and pretty soon we got a deal."

"So Sam's not the jealous type?"

"I didn't say I've been giving it away or selling it since I met Sam."

"You didn't have to."

"I'm 32 and been fucking for more than half my life. I used to do it for fun. Now it relieves boredom or gets me by. That's the way it is for most chicks by the time they get my age. It's better for female cops?"

I say nothing. She continues, "Sam's as okay a guy as I've been with. That means he's a dickhead. When I was a kid I did only white guys. But they're insensitive brutes. Fuck you bad, doze off. Beat you or ignore you until they're ready to get it on again. In between they're tryin' to fuck anything that walks. And sooner or later you get the crabs or chlamydia or somethin' worse. So I switched to the black guys. That's how I got into Howard. And after a few 'Baby, you're the best. I be your man...' bullshit, you get the 'I'm the best, ain't I, baby?' Then they doze off or beat you or go out and hit on other broads and beat you if you bring it up, and sooner or later you get chlamydia or herpes or crabs. Men, black or white, they're all the same."

She rambles. Fine with me, since I recoil about asking the key question: the circumstances surrounding the death of a child about the same age as Liam. I wince as I think of Liam not being. I can't bring myself even to mentally articulate the word "dying." On the other hand, if—God forbid—Liam did cease to exist, I cannot by the wildest stretch of my imagination imagine myself acting and talking like Lilly Higgins. But I finally get to: "You lost a child recently?"

Lilly focuses. "You here for Precious or Howard?"

"The two could be connected."

31

"I told those two cops, the man and woman, all I know. They don't see murder."

"Howard did."

"Who told you that?"

"Several people."

"Yeah, like his Mom, who's addlebrained, and his sister, who's too busy turnin' out kids and rippin' off the taxpayers to have a real thought."

"What happened?"

"Check your records. Precious pulled a pot of boiling water on top of her. The shock killed her."

"Did you see it?"

"I was in the living room. I don't like to talk about Precious. I got feelings. Maybe I should show them. I got that part kicked outta me a long time ago. But it still hurts."

A key turns and the door opens, followed by several seconds of belching, heavy breathing and heavier footsteps down the short hallway separating the front door from the living room. A bulky man not much taller than me, both vertically and horizontally, enters the room. Stringy, dirty-blond hair and three- or four-day stubble cover much of his face, arms bulge through a sleeveless shirt and a ponderous belly extends from his mammoth chest and slightly over his grimy jeans.

"What the fuck this broad doin' here? I hope to Christ you ain't fuckin' around on me, bitch."

"She's a cop, asshole."

"You got a search warrant, bitch?"

"I'm not searching. I'm asking questions."

"I answered every fuckin' question them asshole cops asked. That ain't good enough, so now they send another broad. Shit, lady, you here by yourself? No backup? What if I should swat the shit outta you? Whaddaya gonna do 'bout it?"

"Put a bullet in your head."

"Yeah, yeah, even the broad cops talk tough, as long as you got a piece. Take it off, see how tough you are."

Compared to Sam—whose last name I ultimately discover is Nichols—Lilly is a cross between Miss Manners and a rocket scientist. But I'm used to this kind. When I worked the squads, I'd encounter them at four a.m. Sunday mornings as the drinking establishments closed. I don't know what type of guy Howard was, but he had to be a prince compared to Sam.

"Sam, just shut up," Lilly says.

"Oh, now you're the big, tough pussy. I suppose it's because this chick is sittin' here with a badge and a gun. But she's gonna be gone soon enough."

"Sometimes, Sam, you can learn a little and stay out of trouble if you'd let the other person do the talking before you go start blabbin'. The lady here wants to know about my dear ex-common-law husband's death. She's not interested in Precious."

Sam looks befuddled. "Someone got to that little son-of-a-bitch?" he finally spits out.

"Maybe," I say.

"Whaddaya mean?"

"We're not sure how he died."

"He was a nasty, rotten, sneaky little spade. I ain't sheddin' no tears for him."

"You had a lot of affection for him."

"Huh?"

"He bothered me. Was jealous. Sam didn't take to that," Lilly says.

"How did he take to his daughter's death?"

"He went to the funeral."

"He questioned the cause of her death?"

"I thought you weren't interested in Precious?" Sam asks.

"Shut the fuck up, Sam."

Sam looks at her half-crazed, but backs down. "Fuck you," he says and disappears into the kitchen.

"Everyone had questions about her death. I still do. Why did I leave the kettle so close to the edge? Why did I leave the handle sticking out? Why did I leave Precious alone in the kitchen? Why? Why? Why? Yeah, Howard was upset. He wasn't much of an old man to me, and he didn't much support the kids, but he loved them. He got pissed off plenty and blamed me and Sam, particularly Sam. But Sam didn't put the water on. I did. And Sam loved the kid as much as Howard. But Howard didn't bother us much recently. And we didn't kill the asshole over it."

"You speaking for Sam?"

"Sam's bark is worse than his bite. Down deep he's a big pussycat."

At that point, the pussycat reenters the room, slurping from a can of beer that his meaty paw envelops. "You finished, cop lady? Me and the little lady got some gettin' on to do. Hee, hee, hee." I look at Lilly, who doesn't seem out of her mind with lust, and certainly not starry-eyed with love.

"I don't want to get in the way of good times." I begin to leave, and then realize that I haven't seen the five-year-old, Asha. "Where's your daughter?"

"She's fuckin' dead, remember? We just been talkin' about it!" Sam bellows.

"For Christ's sake, and for the last time, Sam, shut your fuckin' mouth." He throws his arms up in the air, spilling beer, and stomps back into the kitchen. "You're talking about Asha?" she asks.

"Yes."

"The social workers have her."

"The social workers?"

"Yeah. CFS."

"Why?"

"They said after Precious' death, I should have some space, get my act together. And they also said Asha needed grief counseling. They're right. I have my baby's death to deal with, along with handling that big baby out there. It was too much. I was coming apart. So the social workers suggested and I went along. She's been with the state since Precious died. It's okay by me. I get to see her a couple of times a week. She'll be back soon."

"You go to Juvenile Court?"

"No. Strictly voluntary."

"You getting counseling?"

"A little."

"Where's Asha?"

"Can't say."

"Who are the social workers?"

"Can't say."

"Why not?"

"The social workers told me not to tell anything to anyone. It's about confidentiality."

"Even to the cops?"

"To everyone."

"So I guess that's about it. I'll leave you to Lover Boy."

"Yeah, thanks."

Yes, I think, I know all about boring sex; but at least Jeffrey has smarts and manners. Then again, he could use a little—just a little—of Sam's sexual aggressiveness. "How long have you lived here?" I ask as I get to the door.

"Maybe six months."

"Before that?"

"On Kedzie and Irving, a three-room flat over a bar."

"How long you and Sam been together?"

"A couple of years."

I look around the spacious living room. Four windows overlook the street. The furniture is modest but clean. The two bedrooms and a bathroom face a long hallway, and the kitchen and dining room are to the rear. The neighborhood is dicey but the flat is not half-bad.

"Sam work?"

"When he's lucky and ambitious—a rare combination. But he's not illegal. Check your records."

I start the car and Lilly and Sam vanish from my mind, replaced by Andrew. Perhaps when I next see him, he will touch my bare arm. Perhaps we will embrace. Even kiss. I go goose-bumpy with excitement. A touch, a kiss, an embrace need not be adultery. Merely friendship-plus. Plus what? Plus the beginning of a long tortured road leading to regret. But regret of what? My children, of course. I cannot live without them. But then, where does Jeffrey fit into the equation? And if I do not even consider him, how can a touch or kiss or embrace lead to regret?

I take about twice the normal time to negotiate the several miles between Lilly's flat and Headquarters. Traffic, the automobile kind, is light; but the traffic racing through my mind causes me to drive

35

slowly and erratically. I turn in my unmarked squad, wash up and then sit in my own car for many minutes. The hour is late. Liam and Emily most certainly will be in bed by the time I get home. Just Jeffrey and me. I phone anticipating voicemail but hoping differently, and differently it is. "I thought you forgot about me," Andrew says.

"I thought I'd be talking to a recorded Andrew Malcolm."

"You solve the case?"

"Getting there, very slowly."

"Come. Tell me about it."

"Now? At your office?"

"There'll be plenty of company."

"Twenty minutes," and I hardly believe what I have said.

Sixty floors above Michigan Avenue, his office hums like midday with young, well-dressed men and women scurrying down hallways and darting in and out of offices.

"You work in shifts?" I ask as he pulls a bottle of Pinot Grigio from a small refrigerator.

"Inflated rent and inflated salaries add up to inflated hours. Most of the kids out there are young associates several years removed from law school. If they intend to make partner, they must demonstrate their legal acumen. Bill. Bill. Bill."

"And when they make partner?"

"You're either a star or a rainmaker, or both, if you want the big money."

"You're both?"

"The business side of law is more boring and disreputable than the legal side. I dread discussing it."

He hands me a glass of wine. I watch him from the rear as he moves to the open door. He wears a light blue, very smooth button-down shirt with a loosened maroon silk tie. From the rear, he is broad at the shoulders and narrow at the waist, hips and butt. He closes the door and turns around. "You're in great shape," I say impulsively.

"Tennis and racquetball. And you?"

"Chasing bad guys and hyperactive children"

He lounges in a chair across a coffee table from a couch that I occupy. Neither of us speaks. He sips, then gulps his wine. I taste it and put it on the coffee table. I look out the window at the dark expanse of the lake and the glittering occasional lights in Lincoln Park running adjacent to the lake. Just to the west of the park lies the glitter of the Gold Coast.

"You're pensive," he says.

"I was thinking about you."

He stands, refills his glass, walks around the coffee table and sits next to me. He swivels so his knee is propped up over the couch. His hand fingers my hair and then caresses my neck. I close my eyes and soak up feelings that I haven't experienced in years. I don't want him to stop. I want him to move me gently to a supine position. Unbutton my blouse. Undo my jeans. Remove my bra and panties. Caress my legs. Thighs. Arms. Shoulders. Breasts. To make gentle but passionate love.

I touch his face, hand and open my eyes. Smiling at me from a large picture behind his desk are a blonde woman about my age and three children. I leap from the couch.

"I'm so sorry," he jumps up and reaches out to me. I back away until I'm at the window. I want to walk through it. I'm fouling up my life, compromising my vows to Jeffrey and shudder when I think what I could be doing to my children. And what about that woman? Those three smiling children? I shake with shame and disgust.

He touches my shoulder. "I'm sor..."

I turn. "No. I'm sorry. I've led you on."

"Don't be crazy. You've done nothing. I was...overwhelmed by the moment. It won't happen again."

I put my hand to his lips. "No. I'm glad you were overwhelmed. Would I be seeing you weekly for lunch if you were a hotshot female litigator? I think not. I enjoy our time together, our conversation, your touch, too much. I have another life. A husband, children, responsibilities," and I say softly, "vows. And so do you. And maybe you're bored or frustrated or ambivalent with and about your spouse, as I am. But this...This will only make matters worse. Or maybe I'm just a conquest—a different lay—in which case, I'll be even more traumatized."

"My God. How can you even think such a thing?"

I pull away and walk to the photo. "I'm ignorant about a very important part of your existence, as you are of mine. Tell me about her." The juices, his and mine, ebb as he speaks.

"Jennifer volunteers a couple of days a week at a temporary shelter for abused women, is a social worker by profession but doesn't have a paying job. The kids: fourth grade, second grade, preschool. Two girls and a boy."

"How did you and Jennifer meet?"

"Our families summered near each other on the Vineyard. But she was just a kid. Then a few years later I ran into her in a bar on Second Avenue when I was in law school at Columbia and she was at NYU. The rest is history—16 years of history.

"And you? I know your husband Jeffrey teaches English literature. You have two children, Liam and Emily. You've told me all that. But I still know nothing about that aspect of your life. In truth, I don't want to. I don't want to picture you sitting down to dinner with a man who's not me, or being intimate with him. I know that we have different lives, different responsibilities. And I'm mature enough to recognize that we make decisions when we're very young that may be stupid, shortsighted and immature. But children, extended family, finances, loyalty, if not a stupid vow lock us in.

"Okay, Carol, I'm locked in. You're locked in. Does that mean all the passion, all the fire dies with the responsibility? Look at Jennifer. Look at her hard. You feel guilty. Not me. And I love the woman. I love her because at one time, 16 years ago, I was passionate about her. I love her because she's a good mother to three kids I'd give my life for. I love her because for 16 years she's endured me, my idiosyncrasies, with patience and humor.

"We, Jennifer and I, are a finely tuned corporation. We raise kids pretty well. Pay the mortgage and country club fees, go on vacations as a family. Once or twice a year my wife and I go off by ourselves on long weekends—New York, San Francisco, Montreal—where I'm forced to see plays that I hate, go to art museums that I detest, and where she rummages through galleries while I sit in cafés reading a book or a deposition. My existence, our relationship, is cerebral, rational. Money, children, work."

I sink into the couch. I want to tell him that his feelings mirror my own. I won't. His marriage. Mine. And maybe most lose the fire, the irrational passion, the animal in favor of the cerebral. But perhaps this is the only way. I've seen up close relationships where people are irrational, close to animal. I suspect that when they're not killing each other or beating each other up, they have similarly irrational, similarly uninhibited sex at least when they're not too drugged out or boozed up to perform, much less enjoy it. And while they're getting it on, their kids are getting screwed, they're losing jobs and building quite a relationship with state social workers and Criminal Court judges.

I stand, slip on my jacket and walk to where Andrew sits brooding. I kiss him softly on the forehead.

"I'm sorry," he stammers, standing and taking a step back. "I got carried away."

I step toward him. "I'm not sorry." I find his hands and hold them. "We just can't." Though with every cell in my body I want to. Indeed, if it were just the sex, I might. But if I give myself to Andrew it would mean that I love him, or think I love him, or want to love him. Worse, it must mean that I do not love Jeffrey. I take my leave.

I quietly let myself into our dark home and go right to the bathroom. A few minutes later, I have my clothes off, my nightgown on and try to slip into the bedroom unheard.

"Carol?"

"Yes."

"You don't have to be so mouselike. I'm awake." Jeffrey turns on a 25-watt lamp next to the bed. "This case must be something."

"In the scheme of cases, no; but he's a dead guy and he's *my* dead guy."

"And you're going to make the most of it?"

"That's what pays half the mortgage."

"You're a perfectionist."

"How are the kids?" I ask, sitting on the edge of the bed.

"Wound up. I thought they'd never go to sleep. Jumping from bed to bed. Running around the house."

"So what did you give them for a bedtime snack?"

Jeffrey looks guilty. "You weren't here, so I figured they deserved a treat. Cookies and ice cream."

39

"You wonder why they're wired?"

"All's well that ends well, even if it kept me from a few papers."

"What's that supposed to mean?"

"Huh?"

"You're a self-sacrificing New Age male martyr, taking care of the kids while I while away the evening, and a lot of other evenings, not getting to know my kids. In other words, I'm not a good Mom because I refuse to sacrifice my career to spend more time with them."

"Christ, honey," he says softly. "You're on edge." He rolls over to my side of the bed. He self-consciously kisses my thighs. Disgust, shame, guilt. Andrew's touch drove me half-mad with desire. Jeffrey's kisses leave me ice.

He sits next to me and slowly massages my neck and shoulders. He runs his lips along the back of my neck and shoulders and sneaks his hands under my nightie where it comes to rest on my breasts. Despite 13 years of lovemaking, he's still awkward. I try to respond to his advances. But I think of Andrew and our evening together. I compare poor awkward Jeffrey to Andrew, whose soft touch exploded a dormant passion to the surface of my being.

But how can I compare the two men? Andrew: tall, strong, good-looking and rich; Jeffrey: a middle-class college professor, whose 5' 10", 160 pounds, brown eyes and bushy but thinning dark brown hair will never pass as Hollywood—though in fact, at one time I raced home just to be with him. But if I had to share the bills, kids, vacations, extended family obligations with Andrew, maybe his looks and touches wouldn't do much either. Jeffrey may be awkward and lack Andrew's finesse; but he takes good care of the kids, helped me through two pregnancies and saw me naked and bloated on the delivery table.

I turn and roll over on Jeffrey. Suddenly Jeffrey becomes Andrew, and I attack him as I have never done before. When we finish he props himself up on an elbow, runs his fingers through my hair and says, "We've got to do this more often."

"Great, Jeffrey; now I need some sleep." I roll over and grind my teeth. I almost said, "Great, Andrew."

CHAPTER 3

Six hours later, I shower, dress, get the kids up, wash, dress and feed them so Jeffrey can bring them to school and the babysitter. I'm strapping on my holster as Jeffrey comes up behind me and kisses me softly on the neck. "Maybe again tonight," he says.

"No, I should be home early," I reply, purposefully misconstruing the implication of his statement. I turn around and kiss him quickly on the lips. His puppy-dog look pisses me off—only because I feel so guilty.

I kiss the kids goodbye amidst Liam's wails of, "No go, no go!" Emily screams that she's sick and about to die, and Jeffrey bribes them into tranquility with an offer of Sweet Goody cereal, which is supposed to be a Saturday-night treat.

On the way to Headquarters, my pager beeps. It's Andrew. "Let me count the ways," he begins.

"What?"

"The ways you have ensnared me. Beauty, brains, personality, wit, charm..."

"Cut it."

"Seriously, Carol. I wanted to tell you how embarrassed, even guilty I..."

"Andrew, I want to see you again. We can trust ourselves to do the right thing," I say, knowing that perhaps we can't. "But I don't know when. Keep in touch."

Demitra Thanos, a Mediterranean-complexioned, smooth-faced woman about 40, with dark, slightly greying hair, a little shorter and heavier, particularly around the hips, than myself, leans against a cart bearing the body of a large woman. "Your friend

41

drowned. That blow to the head no doubt assisted the process. That was a fresh wound, and one that certainly would render him unconscious, close to death."

"Could he have fallen — say, on the rocks—hit his head and rolled into the lake?"

"Sure—but given the nature of the wound, I suspect that some very strong person used Mr. Pore's head for batting practice. My conclusion is death by drowning brought on by unconsciousness due to a severe head trauma, probable homicide. Anything else?"

"I need a report on a kid autopsied here a couple of months ago."

"The records department is one floor up. They'll pull the documentation."

"Thanks." I turn to go.

"Wait a second—not that little Pore girl?"

"Yes, Precious Pore."

"I didn't make the connection. I don't believe in the death penalty, but I would make an exception for whoever did that."

She brings me to her office, where she spreads a file across a table. She picks up her report and reads, "Unclothed, malnourished, slightly dehydrated-appearing body of a 32-month-old female child weighing 30 pounds. There is an area of third-degree thermal burn with bulbous formation and skin sloughing on the anterior aspect of the genitalia, within the inguinal folds, extending into the perineal area, coming to the level of the right lower sacrum and involving the buttocks bilaterally. There is a searing of the skin between the buttocks deep into the folds surrounding the anus, and the skin at the area of the introitus and the vagina is also seared. The genitalia show burns in the external region."

She puts the report down and turns to me. "You understand that?"

"Her vagina and buttocks got pretty badly burned."

"I'd say." She places a picture in front of me. I've seen a few bodies, but when I see this one, I wince and turn away instinctively. When I look back, I study a very slender little girl lying on the morgue cart. The skin around her vagina appears to have been scalded off. A companion photo shows the same searing around her crotch and buttocks.

Dr. Thanos traces the outlines of the burns with her index finger. "I'd say that someone stood over the child, who, I suspect, was lying on the floor. That someone poured water from a kettle with a narrow spout quite quickly. As the water hit the child, she instinctively rolled into the fetal position to protect herself. The water continued to pour over the left side of her buttocks." She turns to the next photo. The left part of the butt is badly burned, the right side untouched. "The burns appeared to be at least 12 hours old by the time the child was brought to the hospital."

"What killed her?" I ask.

"Her heart stopped beating. Heart failure. The thermal burns had a great deal to do with death. That was a tremendous shock to the system of such a young, fragile child. Delaying medical attention contributed to a fluid loss, which also increased infection."

Thanos pulls a couple of X-rays from a big envelope. She points to the right arm. "The child's radius and ulna were fractured, probably three to eight months prior to her death. I'd guess caused by blunt trauma."

"Anything else?"

"Slight vaginal tears. Maybe from the scalding. Maybe she injured herself falling." She hesitates. "And maybe someone diddled with her. Given the rest of the picture, it's certainly plausible."

"Homicide?"

"Probably homicide. It's up to you folks to take it from there."

"Could the kid have pulled a kettle or pot of boiling water onto herself?"

"Anything's possible. We deal with probabilities. Only a few splash-type burns on her shoulders, chest and upper abdomen. The nature of these burns indicates water specifically poured on her from a height of several feet. The probability of it happening this way is nine out of ten; the probability of accidental scalding is one out of 50."

"Which does mean a possibility," I say.

"Remote, but yes."

"And the vaginal tears?"

"Someone probing with his finger, even penis; or accidentally, an unusual fall."

43

"But you think the worst?"

"Don't you?"

I head out to Area 10 Homicide, where two detectives named Albert and Flynn are assigned to investigate Precious' apparent murder. Since Howard died on the lakefront, my unit got that case.

Bob Albert and Kim Flynn remind me of Ken and Barbie: he, tall, light brown hair, blue eyes, bushy mustache, a Thomas Jefferson-style shirt with all three buttons opened, exposing a hairy chest. She, about 5' 4", blonde, with eyes the color of the lake on a sunny day, and pleasantly built. They're both about my age, but banter like old-timers.

"So someone offed Howard the whiner," Albert drawls, his booted feet propped up on his small metal desk. "That's one less headache for the force."

Kim chuckles, "Actually, he was kind of growing on me in his own bizarre way."

"How's that?" I ask flippantly. Christ, cops can be such assholes—especially young cops on the make. Pore may have been no prize, but someone killed him without a trial or court-appointed counsel; and at least a few people, even if they're his mom and sister, grieve him.

"His kid, what was her name? Precious," they both snicker. "Christ, some of the names we get," Albert continues. "In any event, Precious met a tragic but not unexpected end, given the fact that her mom is a whore junkie space cadet. Howard bugged the shit out of us. On the horn every day bugging us. Stopped by a couple of times a week. Had lotsa theories, one suspect and no proof."

"You think the child's death wasn't homicide?"

"Don't know," Flynn says.

"Thanos says it was."

"How long you been in Homicide?"

"Close to a year."

"You'll learn about some of our pathologists at the Medical Examiner's Office, particularly Thanos. She's a doctor, but not good enough to work on live bodies; so she sees murder on every corpse she cuts, particularly if it's a kid. Did she do Howard's case?"

"Yes."

"Howard must've had dozens of enemies."

"Any ideas?"

"I'd start with his drug dealer, go to his creditors, then to his pals from the joint; and finally I'd ask the old lady's new boyfriend a few questions."

"Why him?"

"For starters," Flynn says, "he's the fellow that Howard tried to finger in Precious' untimely demise."

"With nothing to back it up?" I ask.

"A father's instinct—not that he was any kind of Dad," Flynn says.

"So, where's your investigation now?"

Albert laughs, points to a gray metal file cabinet. "Right here, along with dozens of other unsolved, never-to-be-solved homicides, may-not-be-homicides-but-accidents or justifiable homicides."

"Where does this case fall?"

They both lean back. Albert speaks. "Could be an accident. Mom's explanation makes sense, even if the burn pattern is unusual. Could be murder; but if it was, we haven't got a witness unless druggie, flipped-out mom decides she's tired of loverboy using her as a punching bag and cheap lay."

As Albert speaks, a husky man with a slight middle-aged gut and dark brown hair, thinning a bit on top, and a pleasant I've-seen-a-lot-of-life face enters the squad room and sits at a desk in the far corner. As Albert finishes, the middle-aged detective spreads some papers out on the desk, looks up and says, "God, you college-educated folks have such a way with words."

"Yeah," Albert says with a hint of meanness in his voice, "we're just silver-tongued devils."

"If you skip the adjective, I'd concur," the man says and goes back to his papers.

"Who's he?" I ask quietly.

"You hear that, Welch? A Homicide dick who doesn't know the famous Tommy Welch, a legend in his own mind."

Welch grunts.

"What about the other child?" I ask.

"Other child? Oh, yeah, you mean…what's her name?"

"Asha."

"Yeah, Asha; what kind of name is that?" Albert asks rhetorically. "The kid wasn't much help. Was in another room. 'Bout all she told us was that 'Precious is in Heaven.'"

"You talk to her in the presence of her mom?" Welch asks without looking up from his work.

"You think we're idiots, Welch?" Albert, clearly no Tommy Welch fan, replies.

"How old is the kid?" Welch asks.

"Four or five."

"So two white police officer strangers interview a four- or five-year-old black kid by yourselves?"

"With a couple of CFS social workers," Flynn says.

Welch shakes his head while continuing to write.

"Who made you a supervisor, Welch?" Albert says. "The last time I checked you were a dick, just like us peons."

Welch looks up. "I agree with half of that last sentence." He goes back to his work.

"Can I see your file?" I ask.

They look at each other. "We'll have to clear it with the chief and the ASA."

"Assistant State's Attorney?"

"Of course. Only the state can clear a prosecution." Flynn says.

"But you have nothing to clear."

Flynn shrugs her shoulders. "Tough case. A dead kid. A trigger-happy pathologist. We aren't taking the heat on this. Let the ASA tell us to drop it."

"Has he?"

"We're still looking into it."

"How?" Welch says.

"Go away, Tommy," Flynn says.

"Who's the assistant?" I ask.

"Lenore Weurster," Albert says.

Welch stands, strolls over and sits on the corner of Albert's desk. "Weurster?"

Albert is uncomfortable. "So?"

"She's not a screening ASA."

"This is a unique case," Albert says.

46

"She's not a felony prosecutor. She's the chief at Juvenile."

"Precious Pore was a kid," Albert says.

"Precious Pore is dead. And unless her five-year-old sister is a suspect, the case belongs in Felony. What gives?"

Flynn stands and walks over and confronts Welch. "Back off our case."

"Get out of my face," Welch says crisply.

"You don't like a woman standing up to you, Tommy Welch?"

"I can't stand cops without balls –– and I don't mean the ones allegedly between Albert's legs." He slides away from her and goes back to his desk.

Flynn replaces Welch on the corner of the desk, but faces me. "The family was involved with the Juvenile Court previously, and because of that, Ms. Weurster was assigned the case." Now Flynn raises her voice. "Lenore Weurster was a crack Murder Task Force prosecutor before her promotion to chief at Juvenile."

"What was the Juvenile case?" I ask.

Both look constipated. Albert says, "I don't feel like talking about it. You know, confidentiality and all that bullshit. See Weurster."

I take his advice and head out to the Juvenile Court. "You're a real contradiction in terms," Weurster says as I barely get into the door of her office.

"What do you mean?"

She throws her head back and laughs. "A female dick." She tosses her body into a high-backed Naugahyde swivel chair and props her feet up on the desk in a way that a generation ago would not have been considered very ladylike, particularly since she wears a tight short skirt exposing muscular thighs. Weurster is womanly, in a *zaftig* sort of way: pleasing-looking, large, strong, with good-sized breasts and broad hips with a similarly wide face and wide-set brown eyes. She has dark brown hair and very light, porous-looking peaches-and-cream skin. But if her body is all woman, her demeanor and language are all macho.

"This Lilly Higgins babe is one piece of work. Got kicked out of high school for giving head for six bits during lunch hour. Arrested for hooking, drugs, theft, assault and deceptive practices. Likes bad boys: Howard Pore, her chocolate treat, and now her vanilla scum, Sam Nichols. You're involved in Mr. Pore's untimely but well-deserved death. Can't help you. I'm not assigned to that case."

"Mr. Pore was upset about his daughter's homicide..."

"Stop there. Nothing indicates that this Precious girl—Christ, what a name—was murdered."

"I have a pathologist's report stating probable homicide."

"Probable. Only probable."

"That's right. But you said..."

"Listen, Miss Detective, I'm the lawyer here. You're the cop." She clamps her feet on the floor and her elbows on the desk.

"That's why I'm here," I say.

"How's that?"

"To get your advice." I feel a bit toady, but you get more flies with honey than with vinegar, as Grandma used to say —though Granny didn't have to deal with Lenore Weurster.

"I have no advice."

"But even if Precious wasn't murdered..."

"I didn't say she wasn't murdered. There's no evidence demonstrating that she was and none demonstrating that she wasn't murdered."

"But Howard Pore thought she was. Maybe one of his suspects—Lilly or Sam or both—did him in."

"Maybe. Maybe not. That's your job."

"Can I see your file?" I ask.

"No."

"Why not?"

"What?"

"Why not?"

"I ask the questions around here," Weurster growls.

"So do I."

"You're not a detective very long."

"Actually I have been, though not in Homicide."

"You're not a bad sort, Carol—I can call you Carol? But learn the ropes. We call the shots, the ultimate shots. I suspect you came up the easy way? Not that I blame you; I'd do the same thing if I had to. Most of these guys—and the lawyers are just as bad as the cops—think with their pricks. If a woman wants to get ahead, she moves her buns, gives them a glimpse of thigh, bends over so they'll catch a little titty, maybe even go out with them and give them a little..."

"I came up the old-fashioned way," I say.

"That's what I said," Weurster laughs, "you came up the old-fashioned way, the way women have come up for years. Shake some buns, show some titty..."

"Why are you involved in the case?" I interrupt.

"What do you mean?"

"This is a homicide. You deal with children."

"And tough cases involving kids. The brass asked me to look into this one."

"Who?"

Weurster swivels in the chair and looks out her window at Chicago's West Side. She shakes her head and speaks uncharacteristically softly. "Come on, Carol. Don't get in over your head. People are on top for a lot of reasons and make decisions for a lot of reasons. People like us go along with those decisions, also for very good reasons."

"Your file might help me, so I'd like to talk to someone with responsibility."

"I have responsibility, and there's nothing in our file to assist you. In fact, the homicide file is practically empty."

"Homicide file? Is there another one?"

Weurster stands. "You're barking up the wrong tree. I suggest that you visit Mr. Pore's associates and family, most of whom value life about the same as you and I do a glass of water."

I take her advice and visit with one of his closer associates, as well as with what remains of Mr. Pore. Soft indirect lighting shrouds carpets and furniture a little too long in the tooth. Tall Art Deco lamps guard the flanks of an open coffin, in front of which stands the only living soul, other than me, in the room. She bends over her son's body, running one hand through his hair and clutching his shoulder with the other. She looks at me and then back at Howard. "Howard was a wonderful boy. And believe me, Miss, he wasn't a bad man. But right now, I don't remember him as a man—just as a beautiful little boy. Always smiling, always laughing.

Not a mean bone in that boy's body. And smart! Oh, that boy was smart. Nothin' but As in school. And he loved school."

Her eyes, red, moist, seek comfort and explanation from me, a homicide detective trying to make it in a tough—artificially tough—world where women must out-steel men. I look at this woman and her child, and my own happy-go-lucky, ever-smiling and intelligent Liam confronts me. I take her in my arms. She sobs and cries out; and then from some desolate inner region, she howls, almost like a wolf. Her cries resonate with loneliness, emptiness, anguish, defeat, leaving me shaking with a sense of dread—my stomach churning, heart pounding, head exploding, my soul perhaps understanding for the most fleeting of instants the enormity of what lies beneath the surface of what we choose to see in the Jeanette Pores of the world, of the crushing weight that they bear, the "poetry" of her world.

We stand, arms around each other, for about a minute over the coffin. Finally Mrs. Pore pulls away. "Thank you, honey. You're a very kind, very good woman."

"I want to help," I say, never feeling more helpless.

"Thank you, dearie. Thank you." She shakes her head and wipes away tears with a large meaty hand. "But they'll never let you arrest who really done in this boy."

"Ms. Pore – Jeanette—I want justice for your son. Please help me."

She looks at me sympathetically. "It's too late for justice."

"Then vengeance."

"Yes," she says almost absentmindedly, "vengeance; but against who?"

"Who killed your boy."

"That too."

"Can you think of anyone who can help, fill me in on Howard's concerns over Precious' death?"

"Precious?"

"Howard's daughter."

"She died just like Howard. Murdered."

"Howard thought so. He must have told you or someone about his suspicions?"

"Howard told me that his former lady and her filthy boyfriend tortured little Precious."

"Did he go into detail?"

"No."

"Did he talk to anyone else?"

"Maybe his lawyer."

"He had a lawyer?"

"No, a Public Defender."

"Why?"

"For his case."

"Where?"

"At that big white building."

"Juvenile Court?"

"That be it."

"Why?"

"Dunno. Shouldn't have been there."

"Did the state say that Howard neglected Precious and Asha?"

"No. They say Lilly and her fat boyfriend be neglecting the children. But they charged Howard. Don't know why. He didn't even live with them. I went down the court with Howard. I tried to tell 'em that Howard not even livin' there. They wouldn't let me talk. They say Howard and Lilly abused the kids 'cause the place that Lilly and the fat guy be shacking in be loaded with trash and no heat, and they usin' Lilly's welfare check for drugs and beer. And Asha have some strange bruises. She sayin' she fell down, but I sayin' the big honky be trashin' her."

"So what happened?"

"Dunno. The social workers tell the judge that they're on top of everything. And the judge just continued the case. We go back again and the judge, he says everything is okay and just stops the case. Says the kids are well taken care of. Tells us not to come back. Everyone in the courtroom agrees—everyone but me and their Daddy, who lays in his coffin 'cause he tried to stick up for his own. But they payin' no attention to us niggers, even though the judge and one of the social workers be black."

"You say Lilly's apartment was a mess?"

"Weren't fit for rats, or so I'm told."

"Where'd they live?"

"Off Kedzie, up north. They moved to Uptown after the case be open."

"Been to the new place?"

"Weren't to the old one. Lilly don't care much for her colored relatives."

She turns back to Howard's corpse and places her left hand on his head and runs the back of her hand over his cheeks. "You were such a good boy, such a smart boy, such a funny boy. What happened to all that? Dear God, why did he have to go and grow up?"

Jeanette Pore has forgotten all about me. I quietly leave.

CHAPTER 4

Juvenile Court is a massive steel-and-glass building several miles west of Chicago's Loop. The halls are jammed with potential lifers strutting about with adolescent bravado, harried-looking, poorly dressed women about my age, young kids, toddlers and infants squired about by social-work-looking types. The lawyers in lawyer suits stand out. I go to the PD's office and ask for the name of the lawyer representing Howard Pore and get the "We can't confirm or deny that we represent or did represent such a person without that person's permission or at least without the Assistant Public Defender's say-so" speech.

"Howard's dead, murdered, so I can't get his permission. And I can't get the PD's permission, since it's his name that I'm seeking." I get a blank stare from the rotund woman behind an official-looking desk, and then, "We don't represent Mr. Pore. Can't represent a dead man."

I give up and go to the Clerk's office, where I get the same confidentiality runaround. Finally I find a police squadroom, and the sergeant checks the computer. He informs me that Judge Ronald Roostman heard the case.

The vestibule to Roostman's court is crawling with lawyers and social workers, who far outnumber the parents and kids. After 20 minutes of sparring with lawyers darting in and out of the courtroom, I finally corner the PD supervisor. "I represent 300 parents, my two associates more. I can't remember who I represented yesterday, and won't know who I will tomorrow until a few minutes before the case is called. Naw, I don't remember a Howard Pore." He tries to get past me, but I block his way.

"Your client is dead, probably murdered."

"So?" he asks.

"I need your help."

"I can't tell you what I don't know."

"He was a thin black guy."

"Look around."

"His common-law wife was white."

"Happens."

"She had a big white biker boyfriend. They're both on crack and booze."

"Sounds like a dozen cases I had last week." He pulls out a yellow pad. "Give me your phone number. I'll check the files after court. If Roostman heard it, either one of my associates or myself represented the Dad. I'll check it out and get back in touch with you."

"What kind of judge is Roostman?" I ask.

"Political like all of them, but fair. A gentleman. Sorry, no time to rap. Call you tonight or tomorrow."

I'm just outside the building when the PD catches me. "Detective Moore, I think I do remember your case. The mom was...kind of good-looking in a slinky sort of way. Her boyfriend was a big loud slob who kept butting in."

"Sounds like the happy couple."

"It was a Community Bound case. That's the unit that keeps families together. The case sticks out because in most of these cases the parent or parents, when there are two of them, are for it. In this case, the parents were separated. The mom had a court-appointed lawyer and we represented the father. In most cases there is no dad to represent. In this case there was a conflict, because dad didn't want the child living with the mom and her boyfriend.

"I shouldn't say this, since we represent parents and the Community Bound workers support our clients, but the workers in this case are...how can I put it?...on the far-out end of the spectrum. Believe there's no such thing as a bad parent, particularly if the parent happens to be poor and strung-out. The workers claimed that the dad was jealous, that the mom and her boyfriend were off drugs and had gotten their acts together. They're supervisors with a lot of credibility with this particular judge."

"What is Community Bound?"

"Helps keep families together. Most of these parents aren't bad folks, just overwhelmed. Community Bound helps them get decent housing, bus tokens, even gets them to appointments. Sometimes gives them a little bread, employs homemakers to clean the house, cook, babysit."

"Do you know what happened to the baby, Precious?"

"No. Roostman continued the case for a year. The workers can bring the case back if necessary."

"Scalded to death. The Medical Examiner's office said that it was homicide."

The Public Defender looks like someone slugged him in the stomach. He shakes his head but nothing comes out. Then he mutters, "Son-of-a-bitch. I'm gonna nail those lying sons-of-bitches. I'll get the file tonight. Call me about 8:30 in the morning."

"What can you tell me about the social workers?"

"Jena Joslin and Patty Pearson. Not bad people but true believers, willing to bend or shade their testimony to fit the contours of their philosophical beliefs. And this comes from one who believes Community Bound is a good program and a good idea, as long as the parent is kosher."

"Where do I find them?"

"Their office is on the first floor of the CFS shelter for teenage wards with kids of their own."

On the way to the shelter I get paged by the man I should love but fear I may not. "We've got to do something about Emily."

"Sick again?"

"The school secretary phoned. Emily claims she's dying. Stomachache. I went to the school and had a little chat with her. She says that the teacher is mean and gives her a stomachache. We should see the principal."

"Where is she now?"

"She agreed to stick out the day."

"In exchange for?

"A treat."

"Jeffrey, what was the bribe?"

"A trip to Toys R Us after school."

"We can't afford a toy a day. Besides, she's got to learn to deal with school."

"Just today, to get us over the hump."

"Yes and Pavlov's Emily? And what about Liam? He'll go crazy once he figures out that Emily's manipulated a trip to Toys R Us."

"I'll get him one too."

"Great. Two toys for every tantrum."

"It's just first-grade blues."

"Jeffrey, she's had three years of school."

"Preschool a couple of times a week, and kindergarten isn't really that stressful. First grade with a bad teacher can be the pits."

"Emily is not the only kid in the class."

"But she's a sensitive child."

"I'm sure that Emily is not the only sensitive child in first grade."

"But she's our sensitive child," he says with unusual testiness.

"Emily is a sensitive and bright child who always wants her own way. She's throwing a guilt trip at you, and in turn you're putting it on me. I won't be guilted-out. We are the parents. We make the decisions. We'll talk to her tonight and tough it out after that."

"I promised her Toys R Us."

"Last time, Jeffrey—okay?"

"Sure," he says without conviction. "When will you be home?"

"In time for a late supper, I hope. You'll feed the kids?"

"Who else will?"

"It's the job, Jeffrey; I can't help it."

"Even on Vice you didn't work late all that often. I thought Homicide would give you more regular hours. I mean, once the victim is dead, there's not much you can do for him."

"Unfortunately, many potential witnesses aren't nine-to-five types. In any event, I'll be home at a fairly reasonable hour."

As I put the phone down, I realize that I've been daydreaming of Andrew while speaking with Jeff. Christ, why can't I just forget Andrew? Jeff may not be the best-looking, most romantic guy in town, but he's a decent man, a good dad and...But shit, why can't he be more...like Andrew?

A short, stout, matronly African-American woman, Jena Joslin, sits behind one of two large desks in a cramped office. A tall, thin younger blonde woman with large gold earrings, Patty Pearson, sits behind the other. "How did you come upon our names?" Pearson asks.

"Howard Pore's Public Defender."

"I'm not entire sure that was proper."

"We all work for the taxpayers and we all seek justice."

They look dubious. Joslin responds, "We get paid by the taxpayers, but work for and with troubled families. At times, Ms. Moore, the government is the problem."

"I can believe that. But I'm not part of the problem. Someone apparently has murdered the children's father."

"I can assure you that we had nothing to do with Mr. Pore's death," Joslin says, and they both laugh quietly.

I join in for an appropriate several seconds. "Howard Pore believed that Lilly or Sam had something to do with Precious' death."

"Howard was a substance abuser," Pearson says.

"So are Lilly and Sam."

"They were. They're clean now," Pearson replies.

"They're not exactly a commercial for family values."

"Ms. Higgins and Mr. Nichols have had difficult lives," Pearson says.

"So did Mr. Pore."

"So he did, Ms. Moore; but we had almost nothing to do with him. Our charge was, is, the family of Precious and Asha, who at present are Lilly and Sam. I fail to see how we can assist you," Joslin says.

"Did Howard see Asha after Precious' death?"

"Without a court order, we cannot speak about the case. Besides, I don't see the relevancy."

"Asha could have said something to set him off. In turn he might have threatened Lilly, causing Sam to retaliate."

"Assuming Mr. Pore had visiting privileges with his daughter, these visits would have been supervised by us once Asha came into our custody."

"Where's Asha?"

"Ms. Moore, please."

I move on as politely as they. "What did Asha have to say about Precious' death?"

"Ms. Moore, we simply can't without a..." Joslin begins, but Pearson cuts her off. "She wasn't there when the unfortunate incident occurred. She knows nothing. She told that to your two associates."

"Lilly and Sam lived in a filthy, roach- and rat-infested place on Kedzie."

"What's that got to do with the case?" Pearson asks.

"How did they turn it around so quickly?"

"We have a high success rate."

"But Precious died."

"Accidents happen."

"The Medical Examiner thinks it was more than an accident." If I had a knife I could cut the tension into tiny pieces.

Joslin responds, "I read her reports. I disagree."

"Why?"

"She is a physician dealing with physical evidence, which is normally accurate but not always. We deal with human psyches, and at times we err. But we have dealt with the psyches of Ms. Higgins and Mr. Nichols—who, as you say, are not models for family values; but who, despite a surfeit of bad breaks, have made tremendous strides. And neither is capable of killing or torturing a child."

"What about the broken arm?"

"An old fracture. At times a child falls down and breaks something. No one notices. The pain isn't great. It heals by itself. Had this child died in an upscale neighborhood, the Medical Examiner would never have indicated a homicide."

"And the vaginal tears?"

"A fall from a bike. The scalding itself. The other officers understood."

"I do as well. May I see the child?"

"Asha?"

"Yes."

"Why?"

"To get her version."

"You are tactless."

"I don't understand."

"That child has been traumatized. You're a stranger. Besides, the two officers have already interviewed her."

"With you present."

"Of course. The child knows us, trusts us."

"I have no doubt that she relates well to you—but perhaps I could see her with her Grandma present."

"Howard's mother?"

"Why not?"

"Asha is not bonded to her. Besides, you'll need a court order or Ms. Higgins' permission."

"Thanks for your help," I say and stand.

They walk me to the front door. Pearson says, "You seem like a decent woman."

"I try."

"We are in a difficult business. We aren't perfect."

"Who is?"

"Certainly not us, and certainly not our clients. But we try, and for the most part so do they. Some abusive parents are evil. But the vast majority are decent people who may have committed an evil act, or who ignored what their spouse or boyfriend did. I think—I hope—that neither Ms. Higgins nor Mr. Nichols is an evil person. They may have been narcissistically looking after their own needs and ignored their children at one time. But torture? Never. Sex abuse?" She shakes her head. "Out of the question."

I leave wondering if the two aren't whistling their way past the graveyard, hoping, praying that they are correct, and afraid to adequately assess the alternative.

"Mom!" Emily throws her arms around me, actually around my butt. I kneel on one knee and take her in my arms. "Mommy,

Mommy, come see my picture." I stand to face Liam toddling toward me with outstretched arms. "Mommy, Mommy, I wuv you."

I pick him up, his little arms forming a choke-hold on my neck. I follow Emily into the dining room to admire and praise her stick drawings of dogs, cats, moms, dads, houses, clouds, airplanes and children. "This is my absolute favorite. May I keep it?"

"Yes," she giggles and prints 'I love you, Mom' with a blue crayon.

Jeffrey comes out of the kitchen and pecks me on the cheek. He is grilling burgers and making a salad. I go up to our bedroom. The kids bound after me and bounce on the bed as I change into shorts and a tee-shirt. At that moment I wish that I could vaporize Andrew Malcolm. And though Jeffrey's dutiful kiss didn't exactly start a forest fire, would a relationship with Andrew ultimately end up in an identical emotional desert?

I suffer spiritual schizophrenia.

My body craves the passion, fire, recklessness and abandonment that a relationship with Andrew Malcolm promises. But my soul refuses to surrender the quiet, safe harbor of the love that I share with the Jeffrey package. I love the Jeffrey package. But do I love Jeffrey? And will I forego the passion of my thirties and forties to be alone—or worse, stuck with a man I do not love, respect or even like—as I get older? Or should I try to have both the fire and the safe harbor by taking what I need from both men? Can I deal with the conflict, the deception? Or getting caught?

My body rages for the fire of sexual intimacy with Andrew. And even my soul thirsts for the spiritual side of passion and physical intimacy. For a moment I fantasize about being intimate, unclothed, with Andrew. I rationalize that Jeffrey owes—yes, owes—me the opportunity to get from Andrew what he has failed to provide. And if I ever do give in to my desires, will it not be in part Jeff's fault? He will have driven me to it through all the mechanical kisses and nights of technically proficient but lustless, dutiful lovemaking.

We eat dinner. I listen. Jeffrey has always been a talker—verbal, he'd say—and I'm a good listener. But this evening, he jabbers in an almost manic way about his classes, students, the administration and his co-workers. Liam hops off and on my lap as he shuttles between the kitchen and his sister in the dining room. I nod my head as if I'm really interested. Inside I seethe at this man's inanity. Does he really think that he's the only person ever to have dealt with a bumbling bureaucracy, or the only one whom co-workers seek out when they have problems, or that his jokes and brilliance could ever overwhelm anyone outside the stuffiness of academia?

He cleans the table and stacks the dishes. I sip my beer feeling angry and alone. He leans over, kisses me on the temple. "I'll get the kids their baths and put them to bed. Relax. You're stressed."

Go ahead, patronize me. My paranoia runs rampant. Jeffrey's every action, every word forces me deeper into a maelstrom of hatred and disgust funneled back at him. I argue with myself that Jeffrey is merely a convenient reflection of self-directed anger. But why should I get down on myself? I have carried the relationship. Now I teeter on the edge of giving up. And he has placed me there. But then that tiny and beleaguered part of me talks back and the downward spiral escalates.

That night I wear my long nightgown and turn to the wall, ignoring the fact that Jeffrey has climbed into bed naked. He strokes my leg and as he does so, he lifts my nightgown, strokes the curve of my rear and fondles my back, shoulders and breasts. I remain frozen. Finally he turns away.

I'm a louse, of course, but I refuse to let him label me as such. I turn over and move against him. "Is something wrong?" he asks, and now he faces the opposite wall.

"Stress. The job. The case." Of course he doesn't ask me why the case stresses me out; but of course Howard Pore's homicide has not caused my problem. "Have you ever been unfaithful?" I ask him.

He rolls over and puts his hand on my cheek and says, "Carol, what possessed you?"

"We've been together, lovers, for a long time. You must be bored with me."

"Christ, Carol, I couldn't imagine being naked with another woman, or making love with anyone else. I was hopelessly in love with you from the moment I first saw you at the school cafeteria."

"I'm sorry. I worry about too many things," I say.

"Well, my love for you, my fidelity to you should be two fewer burdens."

I say, "I'm sorry," and we make quiet, proficient love.

CHAPTER 5

I'm at a desk by eight a.m. The PD left a voicemail for me the previous evening. "I checked out our file. A couple of items will interest you. Call me after 8:30 on my direct line."

I do. But the person on the other end has a very different message. "Detective Moore, what brings your call?"

"Your voicemail message."

"Oh, that. Yeah, I phoned last night."

"You said you had some pretty interesting stuff."

"I did? Oh yeah, I did. I was a little punchy after court. I exaggerated."

"Let me see it. Could be useful."

"Naw, forget it."

"Let me be the judge of that."

"I can't let you see my file. I have an attorney/client problem..."

"Your client's dead. You can call his next of kin, his mom. She'll agree to let me see it."

"We just got these confidentiality issues here at Juvenile."

"You didn't have them yesterday."

"I wasn't thinking. You'll have to ask Judge Roostman."

"But the case is closed, insofar as your client is concerned."

"Yeah, but you know: confidentiality. Got to go."

I hang up and stare at a dingy, peeling wall. Abruptly, Sergeant Malone comes out from behind his frosted glass door. "Moore, you and I are wanted at Headquarters. Let's go."

On the way downtown, Malone informs me that the captain of the city's Homicide unit had phoned demanding our immediate presence. "Didn't tell me why. Any ideas?"

"My most recent case."

63

"That black fellow washed up on the shore?"

"Yes."

"Doesn't sound like the type of case to interest the brass. Step on anyone's toes?"

"I wouldn't know if I did. Maybe they want to give us a commendation."

He chuckles, "Yeah, and the tooth fairy will be there to give it to us. The brass hustles us downtown for only one reason: to chew us out. They got to be catching heat from the Commissioner, who is catching it from some politician. You and me, we do the real work—which means we'll catch hell."

Captain Robertson – a tall, greyish, dignified black man, about 50—sits rigidly behind a large walnut desk, drumming his fingers nervously as he talks. Besides Malone and myself, Kim Flynn, Bob Albert and another fiftyish black man, shorter and huskier than Robertson, sit facing Robertson. The shorter fellow with the healthy midriff is introduced as Ollie Tate, Albert and Flynn's sergeant. While Robertson speaks, Tate plays with a green feather sticking jauntily from the band of a purple fedora. He looks bored.

"Detective Moore…may I call you Carol?" Robertson goes on after I nod affirmatively. "Carol, you are a young woman with an impressive record. No one at present holds or will hold anything against you. But you must learn to play by the rules.

"'What in the world is that man talking about?' you ask yourself. The Pore case, of course. You're involved in investigating the possibility that Howard Pore was murdered. These two young professionals," he says, nodding at Albert and Flynn, "are looking into the possibility that his daughter, Precious Pore, was murdered under a separate set of circumstances. Neither are confirmed homicides, but in the past several days you have involved yourself in the Pore child's death."

"I was only investigating the father's murder. But his death could be directly related to that of his child."

Robertson seems stunned at the interruption. So does everyone else. He pauses, then continues. "Deaths, not murders. We don't know if either person was murdered. Indeed, from what Flynn and Albert tell me, it appears that the child was the victim of parental negligence at worst. But even assuming that the Pores, father and daughter, were murdered, you must work with Flynn and Albert. Otherwise you could—may have already—compromise their investigation."

"I'm sorry, I..."

He cuts me off with a wave of his hand and continues speaking. "You left two CFS social workers and an Assistant Public Defender with the implication that you are investigating Precious Pore's death..."

"I did no such thing..."

"That may not have been your intention, but you did. They are fine people. They apparently felt used by you. We need their help, particularly the CFS social workers—not only on this case but on hundreds of others. Stay away from them. Stay away from Precious Pore's case. Is that understood?"

"Captain Robertson, what if Howard Pore was murdered because he was raising certain uncomfortable questions? Like why did the judge let a two-year-old child like Precious Pore live with a couple of degenerate losers like Lilly Higgins and Sam Nichols?"

Robertson swivels back and forth, placing his hands together as if in prayer, his voice tight. "You are not suggesting that a judge or these two social workers had anything to do with Mr. Pore's unfortunate demise?"

"But maybe Howard Pore harassed everyone, including the child's mother and her boyfriend, into knocking him off."

"Prove it. But the social workers, the Public Defender, the judge, the Department of Children and Family Services are out of bounds for you. Understand?"

"But..."

"Understand?"

"Captain..."

"Do you understand, Detective Moore?" he asks firmly.

"I don't know how I'm supposed to..."

Robertson stands. The room is very quiet. "You want back in Vice, or perhaps the squad car?" His face is stone, his voice cold.

"I, I..." I stammer, not knowing how to stand up for what I know to be right in the face of a threat to break me entirely. I'm close to losing it, terrified of either bursting into tears or just telling him to fuck off. Tate speaks up: "I think Detective Moore gets the message."

"I think not, Ollie; and I also think you should keep out of this."

Tate stands. "You asked me here, remember?"

"You're their boss!" Robertson shouts, pointing to Albert and Flynn.

"In most respects."

"And what do you mean by that?"

"You told me not 20 minutes ago that you were taking over direct supervision of their case."

"To make sure that I get no more angry—legitimately angry—phone calls."

"So we all understand the game plan? Albert and Flynn work on the Precious Pore case under your leadership, while Detective Moore works on Howard Pore's case under Sergeant Malone's guidance."

"And she'll stay away from the kid's case, CFS, the judge and from every other social worker, lawyer and judge in this state."

"You will do that, won't you, Detective Moore?" Tate asks.

"Yes," I reply quietly.

"See, Robby? Done. Now, let's call this meeting." He gently takes my arm and I stand. So does Malone. Flynn and Albert remain rooted to their seats.

But Robertson wants the last word. "Detective Moore, everything I hear about you, until now, is good. You're hardworking, smart and a team player. We're a team here. Ask Ollie about Tommy Welch: one of the best detectives we've ever had, but a loser making detective's pay and about ready for retirement. Ollie, his former partner, is a sergeant. I used to work in the unit with them. I'm a captain. I will not hold this little fiasco against you. But straighten up. Otherwise you might end up another Tommy Welch.

"Ollie, don't go. Stay here with Flynn and Albert for a few minutes."

Malone and I exit. "You okay?" he asks.

"Yes."

"Robby's an alright guy. But he's got his own ass to protect, just like the rest of us. Cover yours."

"Yeah."

He winks. "Great. You'll get by. Go on ahead, I've got some business. I'll get one of these desk jockeys to drive me back."

I go to the ladies' room, pull myself together and look into the mirror. Do I really need this? Of course I do. I've got to contribute to paying a mortgage, car payments, credit card bills, groceries and insurance. I leave and walk out to State Street. My head gets light and I fight to regain some kind of composure.

"You okay?" Ollie Tate falls in step next to me.

"Sure. Thanks for intervening. You probably saved my job."

"Forget it." He walks toward the parking lot, stops, turns halfway around, takes his hat off, fingers the feather and comes back. "I'm the chief of those two sorry sons-of-bitches back there. And if you ever repeat what I said, I'll make sure you're broken to meter maid."

I laugh. "I'm glad someone else shares my judgment on that issue."

"Robby's right about Welch. One fuckin' smart cop. Never got far on the force, because he doesn't give a rat's ass about these folks down here who bow and scrape to the politicians. We were partners once. Now I'm allegedly his boss," he laughs. "I give him every tough case and he solves them all. Makes me look good. I should have assigned him the Precious Pore case, but I thought it was a no-brainer.

"But stay away from Tommy Welch. He'll lead you astray, down paths the bosses would never approve. He's one bad dude. For sure stay away from the Chili Parlor at 15th and Damen between about 11:45 and 12:30. Welch eats there every day. Good meeting you, Moore. Something tells me you're my kind of cop." He turns and walks off.

CHAPTER 6

Three middle-aged women in white aprons hustle behind a low counter spooning chili from large vats and pouring beer, root beer and coffee. Every seat at the counter is taken, and all but two of the red Formica tables are occupied. The mostly male hard-hat clientele concentrates on the chili, ignoring the social aspects of the noon meal. Welch, reading a paper, occupies the last stool at the counter, in front of a half-eaten bowl of chili and a cup of coffee. "Detective Welch," I say.

"Tommy," he says and stands. "A bowl of chili and a root beer for the lady. Okay?"

"Sure."

He takes his chili and coffee and we go to a table. "Robby give you a hard time today?"

"I guess."

"He's not a bad sort—unless there's heat, in which case he's an asshole."

The chili comes. I'm not hungry, particularly for chili, but I spoon it around. "How long you on the force?" he asks.

"Twelve years."

"Now you're in the big leagues. What did your dad do?"

"Electrician."

"Brothers and sisters?"

"Four."

"Go to college?"

"Yes."

"How long you married?"

"Thirteen years."

"Where'd you meet your husband?"

"College."

"Why the force?"

"I thought it would be an interesting career, particularly for a woman."

"Your major?"

"Theater."

"Interesting. I never went to college, but I took a couple of courses at Kennedy City College. Poetry mostly. I discovered that what I do occasionally as a hobby stinks."

"Why are you asking me these questions?"

"Why you answering them?"

I laugh. "Because you asked them."

"And I ask them because I don't know what else to say, and you aren't talking."

I look at him. His sleeves are rolled up, revealing powerful, hairy forearms. His collar is open; a narrow, hopelessly out-of-date blue cotton tie hangs over a dark-blue denim shirt. His light-green, almost grey eyes are kind. But I stare at them too long, and a hard screen replaces the kindness. "You look more like the girl next door than a hooker."

"But you should have seen me in leathers, a garter belt, three-inch stiletto heels, a flaming red wig..."

"Yeah, and whips and tongs," he laughs, scrapes the bottom of his bowl and sips his coffee. "Tell me everything you know about Mr. Pore and his daughter, their friends, relatives…and particularly their friends in the judicial and child welfare systems."

I talk for 45 minutes. When I finish, he excuses himself and comes back in a couple of minutes. "Middle-aged male disease. Got to pee a lot. You're getting screwed big-time." I wait for the next morsel of wisdom, and hope it's a little more recondite than the obvious. "Someone messed up here and doesn't want it coming out, even if it means that a child-killer goes free."

"Would social workers have that kind of clout?"

"No, but the bosses of their bosses would. Certainly the judge."

"So what do I do?"

"Pursue your leads. Stay far away from anything that smacks of Precious Pore until you hear from me."

"What will you do?"

"You don't want to know."

"Can I trust you, Tommy?"

"What do you think?"

"I think so."

He fiddles with his spoon again. "Kids?"

"Two, first grade and a toddler."

"I remember those days. Lots of fun, lots of work, at least for my wife. I have two sons in college now."

"Your wife work?"

"I have none, now. My ex went to college late, and discovered that I bored her. She works with the elderly."

"The divorce her idea?"

"I guess so. But I did bore her. She expanded her horizons, while I pretty much remained a cop. It's a pretty insular occupation."

"How long you divorced?"

"Seven, eight years."

"She remarry?"

"She had a friend when she left me, but I guess it didn't work out. I'm sure she's involved. She doesn't confide in me much these days."

"And you? Steady girlfriends?"

"For a night, a week, a month. I'm tough to get along with."

"You don't seem to be," I lie, because in fact I'll bet that he makes Jeffrey look like a forest fire raging out of control.

"You seem interested in marital problems."

"Just conversation," I say.

"Or bored?"

"You're pretty intrusive for someone I just met."

"And you seem to want to be intruded upon." His green-grey eyes bore into me.

"Do you take HMO payments for your psychotherapy?"

"All husbands aren't bad fellows." He laughs.

"Neither are wives. But at times we need attention."

"Don't most folks?"

"Except Tommy Welch," I say.

He laughs. "Let's go. I've got to serve the citizens of this fine town."

"When will I hear from you?"

"Whenever."

He walks me to my car. "See ya, kid."

"Thanks, Dad."

I go back to my desk and check my voicemail. No Andrew. I visit Jeanette Pore, who has little to offer other than the name of the woman with whom Howard apparently found some solace during his last days. "Can you help me to see Asha?" she asks.

"When did you last see her?"

"Howard used to see the kids pretty regular. Lilly and her fat boyfriend would just as soon be without them. He'd bring them by here, but I ain't ever seen Asha since Precious died."

"Did you try?"

"No."

"Why not?"

"That's the way it is."

"You're the Grandma. You've got visitation rights."

"How do I get them?"

"I'd start by calling the caseworkers. They'll refuse. Then go to Juvenile Court. Ask to see the judge's clerk. Tell her that you want to see the judge to ask for visits. I think they'll have to put it on the call."

"Won't do no good."

"Probably not. But at least we'll be able to see what the judge has to say."

"I'll get to it."

I visit Howard's girlfriend. She lives on the top floor of a five-story hotel in the worst section of the West Side, the worst part of the city. I flash my badge to a fat, bald, elderly black man who I suppose is some kind of clerk. "Sure you wanna go up there alone?"

"I'll be okay."

He shakes his head, closes his eyes and appears to doze off.

The elevator, of course, is not working, and judging from the garbage piled up inside the cage, I suspect that it hasn't seen an upper floor in years. I trudge up the stairs. Despite the bald fellow's reservations, in such places white women are normally safe except from an occasional harassing remark, since everyone knows that you're either a cop, social worker or crazy. Even so, I unholster my weapon and carry it under the light jacket that I hold.

The trip up the steps is uneventful, except for the foulest stench this side of Hell. Castoff food, puke, piss, even shit clog the steps and landings. But I only have to endure it for a few minutes. Brenda something-or-other, Howard's girlfriend, has to endure it 24 hours a day; though when I encounter her I realize that she won't have to put up with it much longer—a few months, tops.

Brenda is a shade taller than I. Saucer-like, unfocused eyes overwhelm a gaunt face. Her scraggly hair can't conceal open sores blistering on her head and face. Her arms and legs protrude from a short dress like sticks. Maybe she weighs 90 pounds. She slurs her words and hangs onto the door for support. "Come in, sweetie."

A table, cot and chair furnish the seven-by-nine airless room, which reeks much like the stairwell. Crawling things everywhere. "Sit down."

"I'll stand."

"No problem," she collapses on the cot. "Who are you?"

"A cop."

"Oh, yeah. You told me that, didn't you? Whatchya want?"

"To talk about Howard."

'Don't know no Howard."

"Howard Pore."

She scratches her head slowly and rubs a scab from an old track mark on her arm. "Whatchya say his name be?"

"Howard Pore."

"Howard, yeah, Howard. I think I know that boy. Say, you got any money?"

"No."

"I don't believe I know no Howard."

"Let's go."

"Where?"

73

"To the lockup. A couple of days in County will clear your head," I say—though actually, in her condition, withdrawal would kill her.

"Howard in trouble?"

"He's dead."

"He HIV too?"

"Don't know. But someone split his head open with a baseball bat."

Brenda looks puzzled. "Howard was an okay guy, a generous sort. Too bad. But that's the way things be."

"Did he have any enemies?"

She laughs. "Yeah, the guy who hit him upside the head."

"Any ideas?"

"Howard bought drugs now and then. Maybe he didn't pay up."

"Who did he buy from?"

"I'll look into it. Got a card, sweetie?"

I give her one and leave, expecting never to hear from Brenda again. I go across town to visit Lilly Higgins.

Lilly's firm derriere bulges out of a thong. Her D-cup breasts do much the same for a B halter. She slouches against the door. "Unless you wanna pay, you're not welcome."

"You're still not my type."

"You don't know."

"I've got a few questions."

"You're not supposed to be here, you naughty girl."

"I want to talk to you about Howard's friends, his drug-dealing pals, about his relationship with his daughter."

"Listen, chick, I don't got to talk about nothin' to nobody, and you're nobody. I'm gonna sit in here and wait till that big stupid asshole gets home and get me a real good fuck. And you, go fuck yourself." She smiles, steps back and slowly pushes the door until it separates me from her.

I go back to the car and clasp the steering wheel. So Andrew hasn't called. So Jeffrey is a bit bland. At least I don't have to live like Brenda or Lilly.

"Home early?" Jeffrey asks, just barely brushing the tippy-top cells of my cheek with similar cells of his lips.

"Actually, about my usual time," though it's nearly 7 p.m.

"Uh hum." And he opens a book.

The family room resembles Brenda's flat, and dishes from last night and breakfast are piled in the sink. After hugging Emily and Liam and quieting them to a low roar, I roll up my sleeves and begin to load the dishwasher. Jeffrey sidles up to me. "Go change. I'll take care of this."

Sounds good to me, I think to myself, and go upstairs followed by two hyper children. I could have said, "Christ, Jeffrey, why didn't you take care of this earlier? Or do those empty cereal bowls on the table indicate that you fed the kids Sweet Goodies to shut them up? Which of course it did—for about three minutes, after which we'll have to pay for it for the next several hours while they bounce off the walls. Not to mention that they won't eat their dinner, which incidentally I don't see on the stove or in the oven, and which they should have eaten an hour ago."

But if I brought it up, he'd just passive-aggressively reply that he's been so busy, what with my working so late and his responsibility to his graduate students, not to mention correcting exams, shopping and looking after the kids that he just vegged out.

And I'd say that he's not the only one putting out, that I do the cleaning and cooking most of the time, take the kids to school and the babysitter on most occasions and do 100 percent of everything on weekends or my days off.

But I suppose I could also say that I'm spending a lot of time and energy thinking of Andrew; but damn it, as I seethe about Jeff and daydream about Andrew, Liam and Emily float higher and higher, their leaps carrying them precipitously close to the edge of our bed. I shut down the mayhem and go downstairs. I cook up pasta with jarred tomato sauce while Jeffrey cleans the family room. Dinner is uneventful, except that Liam manages to dump an entire plate of spaghetti on his lap and Emily gives everyone indigestion with her constant whining about her evil first-grade teacher.

While I clean up Liam's mess, he pipes up, "No more s'getti. Want 'roni and cheese," which leads me to believe that the pasta ended up on Liam's lap more by design than accident. In any event, Liam settles for a peanut butter and jelly sandwich, leading Emily to protest her unequal treatment loudly. Through it all, Jeffrey advances his opinion of Emily's school and teacher, of Liam's table manners and how good it is to have me home for dinner, as if I am on the road six days a week.

The phone interrupts. "Oh my God! That's terrible," Jeffrey says.

"What's wrong?" I ask as he sits down.

"One of my graduate students, a nice young man, was killed this afternoon in an automobile accident on Lake Shore Drive." He shakes his head, "You never know. You just never know."

"That's too bad," I say. But a mean-spirited thought seeps through my mind: My problems could be significantly lessened if Jeff met a similar fate. My conscience and then my pager distract me from malicious daydreams. I do not recognize the number. Maybe it's Andrew.

"Something wrong?" Jeffrey asks.

"I'll have to make a call."

"To whom?"

"Work-related."

I go to our bedroom feeling flushed—not the in-control, cool Carol Moore that Jeffrey knows so well. Will he get suspicious? Will he try to lift up the receiver? Of course not.

But it's Tommy, not Andrew. "Whadda you doing?"

"What do most moms do at 8 p.m.?"

"Not tonight. Meet me at my place."

"Why?" I ask, wondering if he has other agendas, though he doesn't seem the type.

"You should be dressed in a way not to be seen in public, decent public."

"What do you mean?"

"You met Sam Nichols once?"

"Yes."

"He get a good look at you?"

"Sam is not an eye-contact man."

"That's what I figured: a neck-down type of guy, particularly with a woman like yourself."

76

"I guess."

"Wear something slinky, sensuous, revealing; lots of makeup, particularly around the eyes. That way, even if he got a halfway decent look at you, it'll throw him off. Get a cheap wig, too."

"That's all I wore in Vice. But what are you up to?"

"You're gonna come on to Sam Nichols tonight. He hangs out at a biker bar."

"Tommy..."

"Up to you."

"I hope the hell you know what you're doing. Where do you live?" I write down the address.

"I've got to go out" I tell Jeff.

"This is crazy."

"It's work. Like correcting papers."

"Yes, but not even my students will kill me over a C."

The three follow me up to our bedroom. The kids are giddy. Jeff nags. Emily and Liam bounce on the bed while I pull off my jeans and jersey. I head to the bathroom. The threesome shadows me until I close the door on their collective faces.

I remove my bra, squeeze into a leather miniskirt and slip on one of Jeff's tee-shirts, tying it at the waist. Jeffrey lectures me through the door. "I don't like this, Carol."

"I don't either, but a woman's got to do what a woman's..."

"It's not funny, Carol. You'll get yourself killed one of these days. Besides, I thought you were out of Vice."

I open the door to an open-mouthed Jeffrey, who stammers, "What happened to your idea of law school?"

"And our debts?"

"We'll survive. You get free tuition, and six years from now you'll probably double your salary."

I sit in front of the mirror applying heavy makeup as he jabbers. I slip on the wig and turn around. "Yuck! Mommy's ugly!" Emily opines.

"Mommy's ugly! Mommy's ugly!" Liam echoes.

"You're not going out like that?" Jeffrey chimes in.

"No." I go to the closet and slip on a pair of leather boots.

"For Christ's sake, Carol!"

"Jeffrey, I'm off to work."

Jeffrey throws up his hands. "Where's your weapon?"

"I can't dress like this and pack a gun on my hip. I'll have a backup."

"Just one?"

"I guess."

"What if something happens to him?"

"It won't."

"You're dressed like a slut hoping that moron comes on to you and you're not even armed?"

"What's a slut?" Emily asks.

"Something Mommy is not," I say and kiss her, kiss all of them and am out the door.

Tommy's three-and-a-half-room, neat but spartanly furnished place sits on the top floor of a three-story U-shaped building across from a synagogue. It's walking distance to the lake on a street that still has more trees than high-rises.

"Where's your bedroom?" I ask after giving the place a once-over.

"Interested?"

"It would be incest."

He grunts. "Behind that wall."

"A Murphy bed that comes out of the wall?"

"Yes."

"I thought they went out of style in the Sixties."

"The new owner took them out of the other apartments, but it saves room. Besides, I don't use it for much other than sleeping."

I follow him into a small dining room and we both sit at a table. He takes some papers out of a manila folder and dumps them in front of me. It's Albert and Flynn's file on the Precious Pore case.

"How did you get this?" I ask, stunned.

"Albert and Flynn aren't exactly geniuses. The other day I heard them tell you that the file was locked in their cabinet. It still was tonight when I picked the lock."

"That's illegal."

"You're joking."

"I can't be a party to this."

"Huh?"

"It's a slippery slope. You compromise just a little to justify an arrest, and then a little more until you're as dirty as the person who committed the crime."

"We're not committing perjury or beating a confession out of some mope."

"But you stole a file."

"I didn't steal a file. I took it from the cabinet..."

"Locked cabinet."

"I took it from a locked cabinet, copied it and replaced it. You have the fruits of my labor. It is a police file. And you are a police officer?"

"Yes, but..."

"It's a police Homicide file. You are a police Homicide detective?"

"Yes, but..."

"In the ordinary course of events, can't one cop look at another cop's file?"

"Yes..."

"And in the ordinary course of events, can a Homicide detective view another Homicide detective's file?"

"Yes, but..."

"But in this case, Captain Robertson specifically forbade you from seeing that file or from working on that case. But we both know he was parroting what some politician told him for reasons that aren't legitimate, right?"

"I guess."

"You guess right. And if you go along with Robertson's sin, aren't you just as guilty?"

"I don't know, but your logic certainly sounds...well, logical." I pull the papers in front of me.

"Take your time."

"Have you read them?"

"Of course."

"What do you think?"

"It's your case. Want a drink?"

"We're working tonight?"

79

"Yes."

"Then nothing."

He pours Chivas into a glass full of ice and goes into the living room. I begin reading.

The first interesting page is their interview with Asha:

Visited child, Asha, at the offices of social workers Joslin and Pearson, who were present at interview. They explained that CFS got involved in the case to provide help to family, including relocation to a new apartment, homemaking services, drug and alcohol counseling and intensive social work intervention. According to the social workers, the mother and her companion, Sam Nichols, have made good progress since the Community Bound involvement of approximately a year ago. At that time, the family was living in a filthy apartment. Both children had bruises that the mother attributed to the birth father, who visits regularly. Both mother and stepfather had significant drug involvement. Though the mother and Nichols have made improvement, the workers admit that they both tested positive at their most recent drug drop two months ago. Since then, the parents have failed to appear on two scheduled drops. The workers point out that the parents have no available transportation.

Asha very shy during interview and looked at Pearson and Joslin frequently. The workers said that she needed their support. However, we feel that the workers may have spent too much time with the child before this interview. She was so overprepared. Became confused. Asha said Precious was in Heaven because she fell into scalding water. I asked her how, and she said taking a bath. Pearson then pointed out that the accident occurred in the kitchen. Asha then said that Precious had pulled a pan of water on top of herself. I asked her if she were there. Asha said yes, but then no. The social workers asked her about mom and dad. She said mommy is okay but sometimes daddy is mean. One of the social workers then said you mean black daddy was the mean one and Asha said yes, 'black daddy is mean.'

We then asked what she meant by mean and she said yelling a lot. Sometimes hitting her. She also said that black daddy drinks too much beer. The social worker asked about white daddy and she said, 'Daddy Howard is the nice daddy.'

The social worker pointed out that daddy Howard was the black daddy. Asha then said that the white daddy is okay. Social workers asked if mother ever hit her. She said sometimes but mommy is nice. The social workers asked if the child wanted to tell us anything else and Asha said no.

Based upon our observations, we think that Asha is not a good witness and cannot assist our investigation with credible evidence. However, we also believe that Asha is under the influence of the social workers, who are too protective, and that she should be interviewed alone at a future time.

Another page memorialized a conversation with Howard Pore:

H.P.—child's birth father—phones. Wants to see us. Says has information but admits that he wasn't present at the death. Has no firsthand information. Put him off.

Howard proceeded to phone about half a dozen times before Flynn and Albert saw him. They summarized his conversation in a paragraph.

H. P. here for over hour. Rambled much but had nothing of substance. Said Sam married before, never divorced. Has child. Doesn't support kid. Wife will have nothing to do with Sam because of some incident in past. Says that we should talk to her. She'll prove Sam is a bad actor. H. P. gave us name and address but she's too removed from case.

Sam and Lilly told Flynn and Albert that they were in the living room when they heard Precious scream. They delayed seeking medical care for several hours because they didn't realize the extent and nature of the burns. Both have extensive criminal records. Both have been apparently doing well over the past year. The rest of the file is inconsequential.

I go over the phone logs. L. W. called the detectives on a number of occasions and they called her twice. The detectives received a phone call from a J. R. T. the day after their first call from L. W. On the following day, they received another phone call from a J. R. T. Although they interviewed Howard Pore a week after this, there has been no substantial work on the file after these phone calls.

"So what do you think?" Welch asks and sits next to me.

"Albert and Flynn are either not very bright, or they are taking a dive."

"Both. You figure out why you're gonna see Sam?"

"To find out about his wife and kid?"

"You compromise him. I'll shake him down."

The tavern, appropriately if not creatively named The Biker Bar, is a nondescript, tiny place with a black wooden door flanked by two large windows, also painted black, jammed between two warehouses, one large, one small, in a corner of the near Northwest side that was previously home to Polish immigrants. They lived in narrow wooden three-story flat buildings with basement apartments, worked in nearby factories and unwound in neighborhood bars. The Poles moved to the suburbs to be replaced by Hispanics. Today, the young moneyed crowd is pushing the Hispanics and few remaining Eastern Europeans elsewhere. The old wooden houses have been renovated or torn down and replaced by stone fortresses. Before long, The Biker Bar will be a coffee bar or overpriced restaurant.

The tavern is a lot larger than it appears from the outside, since the building housing the pub happens to be more or less a large entranceway. The real action takes place through a large door that leads into the first floor of the smaller warehouse sharing a common wall with the bar. The many bikes parked out front aren't nearly enough for the mob inside. The Bar obviously attracts a lot of wannabes; but I infer after scoping out the crowd that the patrons are into a kind of scene: sado and slightly-less-sado, since no one seems masochistic. Or maybe it's just macho, more macho, most macho and most macho of all.

A bar runs perpendicular to one wall. A long narrow mirror behind it permits male patrons to flex and stare menacingly at their reflections. The men are either large and muscular, some with protruding bellies like Sam, or sinewy, taut and muscular. The women, outnumbered about three or four to one, are as lean and tough-looking as the men. Both men and women look like they pump iron and chew steroids. The men wear jeans or leathers with dirty tee-shirts under leather vests. A few sport leather vests over naked chests. The women dress pretty much the same, but a few have leather minis and not much else. Most of the women have their hair died jet-black and sport ear, nose and lip rings. I may be the only non-tattooed woman in the saloon. Even with my wig and mascara, I look too much like the girl next door.

Clusters of men and women congregate throughout the room, mostly along the walls. The center is vacant, apparently for dancing to what seems to me to be Fifties and Sixties bubblegum rock stuff.

I glide through the room to more than a few hard stares, hoping that Tommy, who drove separately, is somewhere in the crowd. In one corner I encounter something that I never saw at a whore bar, where arrangements are made but the coupling occurs elsewhere. A guy's bare butt heaves up and down, his jeans down around his knees. A black-haired, hard-looking skinny woman, maybe 25, rides him rhythmically, the front of her miniskirt slightly raised and pressed against his stomach, her hands around his neck. A pair of panties dangles around her wrist. An unseen hand assaults my rear. "That could be us, babycakes."

I turn to face a tough, thin guy with a much-too-small tee-shirt, long, sinewy, strong tattooed arms and jeans. His hair oily, dirty actually. A scraggly eight- or nine-day half-grown beard partially conceals a pockmarked, ugly face. His breath stinks slightly less rancidly than the stairwell at the tenement hotel that I visited earlier.

"Could be you, if you dropped trou, grabbed that tiny thing and jagged off," I say in my toughest street voice. God, if Jeffrey could see and hear his wife at work.

He grabs my throat and shoves me into the copulating couple, who don't seem much bothered by my careening body. "Fuck off, whore. Slut. Cunt. Pussy."

"Quite a vocabulary. Go to college or something?"

"Get the fuck outta here. This ain't a payin' place."

83

"No wonder you're so horny."

He looks puzzled. "I'll give you five bucks for head and six for around the world." He grabs my hair, pulling off the wig. "Ooh, what nice blonde hair." He grabs my hair and tries shoving my face into his groin. "Suck up, babycakes, suck up."

As he grabs me, I push my knee hard between his legs. He howls, lets go and stumbles. I try to get away, but a couple of the ladies and a guy grab me. A crowd quickly gathers. "Goin' somewhere?" one of the gentlemen snarls.

A woman taunts my aggressor: "Gonna let a pussy beat you? Come on, Bobby; let's see what you're made of. Maybe you do have a tiny thing."

Lots of laughing. None from me. I look wildly around the room for Tommy. My aggressor rips his tee-shirt off. "Come get it, cunt."

He lunges at me, but two beefy guys intercept him. "Too many steroids today, Bobby?" one says. They drag him away. The crowd disperses and I pull away. I walk past the two guys trying to calm Bobby down. I see Tommy standing a few feet behind them. He grabs my arm and says loudly, "Hi, chick."

"What's up, asshole?"

"You okay?" he whispers.

"No thanks to you."

"Your rescuers discovered chivalry with the assistance of 20 bucks each."

"Figures."

"Sam's standing with a group just to the left of the bar, but you have competition."

I saunter past the group and get no attention. I stand off to one side, and after several moments make eye contact. His eyes quickly drop to my shoulders, breasts, waist; and then they really light up at my legs. I turn away for a moment or two, and then slowly turn my body around and gradually back again until I face him. His eyes are riveted on me. I slowly sashay past the group and stop right in front of him. "Don't I know you?" he asks.

Hopefully a come-on. "You will if you buy me a beer."

Sam throws an arm around my waist and as he hustles me to the bar, his hand gropes at my butt. We catch daggers from the ladies he'd been romancing. He fondles my buns. "A beer doesn't buy you the privilege." I squirm out of his grasp, but turn my body into his and lean against his large belly. I feel like throwing up.

"A real she-cat."

"Grrr," I say, feeling moronic.

"I'll bet you're a tiger in bed."

I put my fingers to his lips. "You're the tiger, big boy. I'm the tigress. Grrrr."

"Have I won the Lotto or something?" Sam asks no one in particular. "Let's do it now. Over there."

"A tiger and his prey need a lot more room to play. We'll go to your place."

"I, we, can't. Not tonight," he stammers.

"You got an old lady?"

"Me? An old lady? I'm not a one-woman man—at least, not until tonight," he laughs, slobbering beer all over the front of his shirt and my face. "My ma's sleeping over tonight."

"Tomorrow."

"Tonight. Tonight. Your place."

"I have a very jealous roommate."

"Hee, hee, hee," he smirks.

"How 'bout a hotel? A couple rent rooms by the hour not too far away."

"Let's go."

Sam winks at his friends and we leave. Once outside he envelops me in his massive arms, his meaty tongue prying at my clenched mouth. "I thought you wanted some of the good stuff."

"Not in the middle of Grand Avenue. Where's your car?"

"Next block." So much for the social workers' excuse that Sam and Lilly didn't do the drug drops because of a lack of transportation. We go off the main drag to a dark side street. I furtively look behind. No Welch.

"What's your name?" I ask.

"George. Yours?"

"Sam."

"That ain't no lady's name."

"Samantha."

"I heard that once."

"Let's stop for a second," I say when we're about halfway down the block and no sign of Tommy.

"What about the hotel?"

"It'll wait." I grab his belt and pull him to me, feeling more repelled than I can ever remember. But I have to stall for Welch to catch up. Sam's tongue again assaults me. I just can't take it. I push him away and begin to run.

"What the fuck you doin', bitch?" Sam lunges after me, grabbing me as I trip. The leather boots are not exactly running shoes. "Listen, cunt, you want to fuck so we're gonna fuck. No one cock-teases Sam Nichols."

"Up to your old tricks, Sam?" a voice comes from the shadows.

"Huh?" Sam says, startled.

Tommy steps out of a gangway. "I said you're up to your old tricks, assaulting women. Too bad there ain't no little kids for you to lay into."

"Get lost. Like quick, asshole."

"You haven't been convicted of assault for a while. Maybe now's the time."

Sam reaches into his pocket, but Tommy flashes his .38. Sam's hand goes to his side quickly. "Whaddaya want?"

"Police. Turn around and put your hands behind you." Welch tosses me a pair of cuffs. "Put 'em on, lady." I do.

"Let's go," Welch says.

"Where?"

"To your car."

"It ain't here."

"What do you mean, 'It ain't here?'" I say.

"It's on the other side of Grand."

"Ah, so you and the lady just out to catch a little fresh air. How romantic."

"He was taking me to his car," I say.

"He was taking you to a dark alley where he'd probably have raped you."

"That ain't so. I was gonna sweet-talk her into a little head. That ain't illegal."

86

"Let's see what you're carrying." Welch pats him down, pulling three joints from a shirt pocket. "Drugs. My God, I'm shocked!"

"Just fuckin' hash, man."

"Illegal, man."

"Fuck you. No one gets arrested for hash these days."

"You're not no one. You're Sam Nichols. And what do I see here? A pistol."

"A fuckin' .22. I need it down here."

"Registered, I presume."

"Fuck you, asshole. You're a fuckin' smart cop. You gonna make headlines busting me for an unregistered weapon and three fucking joints? I'll see you busted. I got contacts."

"Shall we talk about them?"

"Just talking. You ain't gonna pull me in for a couple of joints and a gun? This lady here and me were gonna have consensual sex, ain't that right?"

"This here ain't no lady. She's a hooker. Right, Star?"

"I guess."

"And I may have saved your life, Sam. She's HIV. Isn't that right, Star?"

"'Fraid so."

"You motherfucker, son-of-a-fucking-bitch!" Sam bellows.

"Keep your voice down, Sam, or I'll club you. And incidentally, what will your old lady—what's her name, Lilly?—say when she finds out that you were soliciting an HIV-infected hooker? She'll probably toss you out—after she removes your dick."

"Fuck you, motherfucker."

"Actually, I'm a nice guy, Sam, and I'm not a bit interested in you, your joints, your whore or your old lady. At least not this one."

"What?"

"The lady you had the kid with, your wife—remember her?"

"Karen?"

"Yeah, Karen. What other names she go by?"

"Just Karen. What she done?"

"That's for me to worry about."

"I ain't the kind to tell stories."

"I hear you got some new worries."

87

"What you talking about?"

"Like the CPD looking into your girlfriend's daughter's death and her ex-boyfriend's murder and you being a number-one suspect in both cases."

"You know nothin' from nothin', Mr. Cop. I got nothin' to do with either case. The cops ain't even investigating no more."

"That's what they tell you?"

"I got sources."

"Well, my sources tell me that some of the cops are trying real hard to put Howard Pore's murder right on your doorstep."

"They better be good. I got an alibi."

"So you must know when Howard Pore was murdered."

"I know I didn't do it."

Tommy walks up to Sam and puts the joints back in his pocket. "Sam, I don't give a flying fuck about Howard Pore or his daughter. I care about Karen and welfare fraud."

"So the bitch is rippin' off the government?"

"Could be."

"Yeah. Get her. She don't mean nothin' to me, anyway."

"When did you see her last?"

"Two, three years ago."

"Your daughter?"

"What about her?"

"When did you see her last?"

"Same time."

"How old is she?"

"Maybe five."

"What's her name?"

"Who?"

"Your daughter."

"I thought you knew everything."

"Her name, Sam."

"Karen, just like her old lady's."

"Last name?"

"Nichols, like mine."

"I don't think so. You never got married, officially."

"Then she'd go by Hanson, just like her Mom."

"Last known address?"

"She lives out in Cicero, Berwyn, Lyons, some place like that. Moves around a lot. But always out southwest."

Tommy walks up behind Sam and unlocks the cuffs. "Get outta here."

"What about the gun?"

"Sam, get the fuck out of here."

He ambles away, looking back at us once over his shoulder. When he hits Grand, he disappears.

"Come on, kid, I'll walk you to your car," Welch says as Sam turns the corner.

I look at Tommy, and suddenly he becomes the focus of every ounce of frustration simmering within me. Without thinking, I slap him as hard as I can across the face. He looks stunned, but manages to grab my wrist as both my hands attack his face. "What gives, kid?" he asks. And I do something that I haven't done since the third grade: I burst into tears.

Welch quickly releases my wrist, and like many men hasn't the faintest idea of how to react to a woman in pain, particularly when that woman is out of control. He puts both his hands on my shoulders. Finally, I pull myself together. "I'm sorry, Tommy. I feel like a fool."

"That's okay. It didn't hurt."

"I'm not sorry I slapped you. You deserved that, and more. I'm sorry for breaking down. That's something I wouldn't do in front of my husband, Andrew, my kids, my parents or any of my partners. All the frustration in this shitty job and in my shitty life just boiled over in the precise moment that Sam Nichols turned that corner."

"Can I..." Welch begins to stammer.

"Look at me," I say, raising my voice to a shout. "I look like a fool. A 35-year-old woman with a husband, two children, a college degree, dressed in boots, a tee-shirt, braless and with not much on below."

"It's part of the job. I don't see..."

"How would you like to prance into a public place, even a public place full of losers, dressed like a teenage prostitute?"

"Well, I..."

"And have some large-bellied, repulsive-looking, foul-smelling oaf fondle your behind and try to shove a tongue no doubt loaded with every rotten amoeba in the universe down your throat? Or have some other jerk grab your butt, choke you and toss you into two fools screwing in a corner and then attempt to pummel you to death?"

"Carol, I..."

"Not to mention all the times I dressed in garter belts, opera hose, three-and-a-half inch spiked heels and stupid-looking skirts and bras to entice some asshole. What if you had to do that, Tommy Welch? What if Malone and Robertson or any of those fools had to?"

Welch takes off his UAW jacket and puts it around my shoulders and hesitatingly puts his arm around me. "Come on, kid, I'll walk you to your car.

"You're right," he says as we walk. "I'd clean up after elephants before I'd go through what you did tonight."

"I'll never do this shit again," I say.

"Don't blame you."

"It's demeaning."

"Yeah."

"You don't seem convinced."

"Oh, I'm convinced all right, but...well, it's a useful tool."

"What's a useful tool?"

"A good-looking woman's body."

"You haven't heard a thing I've said."

"I hear you. But I also know that fools like Sam Nichols can be had by a nice body, a good pair of legs or a firm butt.

Actually, in Sam's case, any kind of legs or butt will do."

"It's not just low-lifes like Sam, but drunk CEOs..."

"Yeah, lots of men follow their pricks into stupidity or worse. And I'll give you this much. No woman would be stupid enough to follow her fantasies into trouble. No, I don't have to prance around in a half a tee-shirt and miniskirt." I begin to giggle, and then laugh.

"What's up?"

"The thought of you like that."

"I wouldn't turn too many women on?"

"Let's just say that if I were you, I'd rely on your mind, Tommy, and not your semi-nude bod."

"Then I am in trouble. Personality?"

"You're in trouble, Tommy Welch."

We get to the car. "When will I hear from you again?" I ask.

"You won't, unless you need me. But I think you've got everything under control."

Sure. Everything under control, like my relationship with Andrew and Jeffrey and my kids and my job. "Thanks for everything, Tommy. I owe you lunch at the Chili Parlor."

"I'll count on it. And by the way, on those rare occasions when you do break down...be careful."

As I put the key in the ignition, I figure out what he's talking about. I told him that I wouldn't lose control in front of my husband — or Andrew. I start the car and glance at my pager. I phone the number, which I don't recognize.

"Carol."

"Andrew," I begin to tremble. "Where are you?"

"At the Sheraton. Worked too late and must be at the office by 7 a.m., so I just had the firm rent a suite. Doesn't make much sense to drive 20 miles, lose an hour and a half sleep at both ends and not see my kids anyway. I'm bored. Figured I'd see if you're making our streets safe this late."

"I'm on my way home."

"How about a detour?"

"It's past midnight."

"A glass of wine, a cup of coffee at the bar in the lobby. I'm asking for 20 minutes...I shouldn't say this, but all I do is think of you. I can't sleep, eat..."

"What about billing?"

"Don't be cruel."

"I'm sorry, Andrew. I'm just so confused."

"I'm pressuring you."

"I'm pressuring myself."

"I have to see you now. Tonight."

"I can't be seen in public."

91

"What?"

"I'm dressed. I should say not dressed. I was on a job. I look like a cheap hooker. I'm almost naked."

"Come up to my room."

"Andrew."

"I won't hit on you."

Of course he will, particularly undressed as I am. But I want to see him. I want him to hold me and then I will leave. I start to say yes, but the negative comes out. "I'm sorry. Not tonight."

"Please?"

"Something bad will happen."

"I promise, no."

"I want it to happen, but it's wrong for me, for you, for our families. We've got to think this through, talk it through."

"Now. Tonight."

"We're too emotional and I am too unclothed."

"God!"

"What?"

"I'd love to see you. Get my hands on you."

"Now you're being honest. We'll talk tomorrow."

"Yeah," he says, not very much unlike a petulant youngster. I have opted not for Jeffrey but for fidelity, vows, abstractions that do not easily get me through confusing days and barren nights. But if I turned my back on these abstractions, would the beauty and joy of passionate, animal sex be ultimately overwhelmed by such guilt and pain as to ruin my marriage, which is at this point a much larger package than just Jeffrey?

I curse Jeffrey for this yoke of fidelity. And what is fidelity but two people sharing their lives, futures, families, children, successes, lovemaking? Maybe Jeff has never cheated with another woman; but goddamnit, he has cheated me repeatedly by his indifference, narcissism and ultimately his failure to provide zest, passion, affection, spontaneity. Real love. Real sex that leaves one — me—exhausted, elated, fulfilled and very much in love. Jeff has been the unfaithful partner. I have remained true to my vows. I will no longer bear the burden. I will have excitement, romance, perhaps sex. And Jeff will have driven me there.

92

I phone Andrew. "I'll be there in 15 minutes. What's your room?" As soon as he gives me the number I disconnect. I don't want to waste another word.

I get through the lobby without being stopped by hotel security or hit on by horny salesmen. Andrew opens the door.

"My God!" he gasps, and I'm in his arms. I pull his face and mouth into mine. I cradle his face in my hands. His hands are everywhere. He shoves my panties aside and grasps my buns. He pulls me deeper into the room. "I've got to close the door."

I want him to close the door. I want him to lead me to the bed. That's why I came, maybe. I guess. But what about Jeffrey? Emily? Liam? I pull away. "I'm leaving."

"What?"

I kiss him again. "Not now."

"Carol." He clasps me to him, pulls the tee-shirt down, licks, kisses, bites my shoulders.

"No." I push him away again.

"But why?"

"We're not ready."

"We're both more than ready."

"Physically."

"What's wrong with physical?"

I'm out the door, down the elevator and on my way home in just a few minutes. I don't know if I've totally compromised my vows, or if I will, but right now I don't feel guilty. In fact, I feel pretty damn good.

93

CHAPTER 6

I slip into the house and then into the bathroom. I wipe off the makeup and brush my teeth, but I'm too beat for the shower. I ease into bed. "Everything okay, hon?" Jeffrey asks sleepily.

"Couldn't be better."

He strokes my arm and snuggles next to me, his right hand stroking my leg and butt. The next thing I know the alarm is jarring me into a new day, just four-and-a-half hours later.

I repeat the morning routine: Shower. Dress. Makeup. Get the kids up, cleaned, dressed. Rice Chex and juice for them and coffee, very strong coffee and an English muffin for me—and for Jeffrey, who probably jokes but I hear whine: "This is one mean cup of coffee!"

"Add water."

"Lighten up, Carol."

"Hee-hee. The humor went over my head."

I'm to work early, but Tommy arrived much earlier or worked much later. A voicemail from him gives me Karen Hanson's address and phone number.

Lyons is an older suburb just southwest of Chicago, with modest homes, trailer parks and mean-looking apartments over meaner-looking bars. Karen Hanson lives in one of those apartments.

The furniture in the small, clean living room is of the blindingly bright polyester-covered variety that appears almost decent in showrooms of marginal stores pushing it at twice its value (actually five or six times the value, by the time the final payments are made by marginal people). Karen Hanson's furniture, though, is probably second-hand, and the polyester appears dingy, bleak and depressing. So does Karen. She's about 5' 4", with hair tinted several shades lighter than its dark-brown roots, brown eyes, a plumpish face probably pretty eight or nine years ago. Her cheap blouse reveals arms too soft and fleshy.

Karen is no Rhodes scholar, but definitely brighter than Sam and a whole lot nicer. "Sam? I ain't seen him in three, maybe four years. And pray to God I never set eyes on the son-of-a-B as long as I live. He was rotten from top to bottom, inside and out. It doesn't surprise me he's in trouble. Told those two social workers all about him."

"Which ones?"

"The white one and the black one. Look like they sucked lemons, like they didn't want to hear me out. So why they come out if they don't want to hear me? They say Sam's okay, but like I said, he's rotten every which way; and they said, how do I know? Like I didn't live with the son-of-a-B off and on for too many years, not to know nothin' about him!

"Yeah, when I first met him I thought he was somethin', but I didn't know from nothin'. I was just 15, him twenty-four, five. My Mom said he was a no-good louse the second she laid eyes on him. Said he was after one thing, but that don't make him no different from than any other man or boy I ever knew, including a couple of Ma's boyfriends. But Sam was different, I thought: "You're my babycakes and I'm gonna take care of you for life." He was great for carrying on, if you know what I mean. We carried on under porches, in bushes, even in a tree once. And I got pregnant and Karen was born before I was 17. She's eight now, goin' on nine. Smart as hell. Didn't get it from her old man.

"And what an old man! Sam and I got a place when I found out I was pregnant. I dropped out of school and got a job at a bar around here. Worked nights, wore shorts and a halter and hustled drinks. Got fired when I began to show. Then waitressed until an hour or two before Karen was born. Sam said he was always lookin' for work, but he mostly hung out, watched TV, snorted and drank and smoked dope and sold a little on the side. I talked to him about his ways and got slugged for my troubles. When I got bloated, Sam stopped comin' home at nights. I knowed he was screwing around, but I kept my mouth shut. Didn't need him hurtin' the baby.

"Once Karen was born it got worse. We lost our apartment and moved into a two-room place that makes this look like a mansion. I didn't mind. I thought Sam would straighten out. Actually, for the next couple of years, Sam was in jail more than out. Then, when Karen was about two-and-a-half, he came back. Said everything was gonna change. I believed him. He sent me back out to work. I was still in okay shape, so I could hustle drinks at some of the crummier bars. I even waitressed during the day. Sam sat on his fat butt, supposed to babysit Karen but watched TV. More than once I came home to find Karen all alone watching TV or sleeping. Sam was out.

"Yet, Miss Detective, I put up with it, even though I knew he was a loser. I couldn't stand to be alone, all by myself, just me and little Karen. But I've been alone now for a while. Actually, not quite. I've had some friends: some okay, some not so okay, but none as bad as Sam.

"And then I found out Sam was dealing out of my flat when I was working. All kinds of creeps comin' up. Karen start actin' funny. Wettin' the bed for no reason. Not saying anything when Sam was around. Acting scared. Sad. She wouldn't talk about it; but one time when Sam was gone for a couple of days, she said Sam had touched her. I about killed him. He denied it. Said some druggie must of done it. Swore he'd stop selling, go straight. No way. No way I'd have the son-of-a-B around my daughter. I kicked him out.

"Yeah, 'course I told the social workers all this. They said I could be wrong. It could of been a druggie, that Karen might have been—what's the word?—manipulating me 'cause she didn't like Sam. That she thought Sam was coming between us. That Karen and I lived together so long that she was jealous of Sam. It wasn't like she's some college-educated social worker. She was only three-and-a-half. And she was old enough to know the difference between that big asshole that she saw everyday and some druggie that comes by a couple of times a month. But the social workers said Sam had changed. He was no longer sellin', or usin' even, or even beatin' up on his new old lady. That's fine, I said, but I just hope his new old lady ain't got no little girls.

97

"No coppers come by and talk to me about Sam. Not recently. A couple of years ago, yeah, after he was arrested for the umpteenth time for selling. I don't know why the son-of-a-bitch never did big time. Just a lot of county jail time. But not quite two years ago he got arrested by the Feds—the narcs, you know. I figured for sure he'd catch his lunch. You know, them Feds don't mess around.

"Can't remember too much about the narcs. One was Mexican, I think, and the other, kinda old and bald. And then maybe a month later, two FBI agents come by. Asked me lots of the same shit the two narcs did, but were a lot nicer. The narcs swore a lot, you know, and shovin' their weight around like their shit don't stink and they were important. They threatened me and my kid if I didn't cooperate. But I told them everything just like I told you, and I told the FBI agents and the social workers. But they said they'd bust me. Like for what? I ain't never did drugs in my life. But the FBI was real nice.

"Yeah, a lady and a man. She had dark curly hair and dark eyes. Maybe about your height. She looked like she might have been Italian or Mexican. He was tall, real tall, with brown hair and kinda nice-looking. Wore gold glasses, metal-like. But his hair was not as dark as hers.

"The whole thing seemed funny: the narcs tryin' to make Sam out for the jerk he is, but pushing me to lie. Wanted me to say I saw him abuse Karen. He did, but I didn't see nothin'. If I did I would of killed him on the spot or be killed tryin'. The FBI was just the opposite. They were almost like the social workers—said not to pay attention to the narcs. Hinted it might be a mistake, that lots of kids act like Karen when she was three-and-a-half. They said that since I didn't go to the cops or CFS, I would look real bad if I tried to say that Sam had abused Karen. Yeah, I didn't go to the cops or CFS 'cause no one was gonna mess with my daughter again."

On the drive back to the office, I wonder about the contradictions. Why do state social workers protect two big-time losers like Lilly and Sam? Why do the Chicago Police Department and State's Attorney essentially take a fall on the brutal murder of a two-year-old child? Why do the Feds protect Sam Nichols?

A good place to begin unraveling these puzzles is Vice Headquarters, where I have friends; and Vice should have microfiche records on Sam's narcotics bust. When I walk in, a short, bald, beefy fellow at the desk greets me: "Collar any drunk CEOs lately? Whatchya need?"

Sam's arrest record is unremarkable, at least for Sam: assault, domestic violence, possession and sale of drugs. But what is remarkable is that he never did penitentiary time, particularly since his last arrest was allegedly for the sale of $50,000 worth of crack to undercover cops. But the case was dismissed. This aspect of Sam's record corroborates Karen Hanson's story. But another aspect of her story doesn't add up. According to the records, Sam was never arrested by the Feds. And if Hanson was mistaken about this arrest, why would the Feds be so interested in questioning her about him?

I pull up the police reports of Sam's arrests. Again, pure Sam. He assaulted teachers, girlfriends, Karen, bartenders and druggies. He possessed crack, marijuana, heroin and PCP. When I get to his last arrest, the sheet shows one word: "DELETED". The screen doesn't tell me who deleted it, why it was deleted or even when it was deleted. Just deleted. I go back to the actual rap sheet, which gives me the badge numbers of the arresting cops. I check those out and discover that both were from Vice. One I know. After a few phone calls, I find Ronny Ramirez at home. "Ronny, can I come by to see you?"

"I win the Lotto?"

"Christ, Ramirez, I heard that line just last night from a slob you arrested a couple of years back."

"Don't be so serious, Carol. Come on by. I'll make you an espresso."

Ronny is a single fellow, a little short of 30 with shoulder-length dark hair and large, soft brown eyes set in a strong, smooth face. If he were about five inches taller than his 5' 6", he'd be my type. He wears pajama bottoms and a strong upper body. "You pump iron, Ronny?"

"I got to do something with my spare time."

"I figure you'd have dozens of women clawing at you."

"Saving myself for you."

"Too bad, Ronny. You have so much to offer to so many women."

"Ah, but the wait for perfection is worth it."

"But you'll be so old."

"Yeah, I probably won't be too good by then."

"So what changes?"

"Unfortunately, you don't know."

"Nor will I ever."

"Poor girl," he says as he pours me an espresso that he has made from one of those little plastic machines. We sit in a sun-drenched kitchen overlooking the el tracks.

"Are you going to the ballgame today?" I ask, knowing that he lives close to the ballpark and works nights so that he can attend most of the Cubs' games.

"That's the good news. The bad is that the season is almost over."

"Ronny, for the Cubs, the season was over in April."

"What do you know about baseball?"

"Enough to know that the Cubs haven't won a pennant in maybe a hundred years."

"See, you know nothing. They won a pennant as recently as 1945. Admittedly they haven't won a World Series in about 90 years. But it's good just to sit in the sun and hope. Winning would be disappointing—nothing to hope for, to anticipate. So, what about this fellow you arrested last night?"

"I didn't arrest him. I was undercover."

"Thought you were finished with that crap?"

"I am, as of last night."

"What's his name?"

"Sam Nichols."

"Don't know him."

"Big guy, not real tall, maybe 5' 9" but wide as a piano. Big arms, scruffy beard, stringy, dirty blond hair, dumb as a rock."

"Sounds like most of the white guys I've collared."

"Two years ago, you and a cop named Smith set Sam up to sell you a couple of kilos of crack worth 50 grand."

Ramirez leans back, clasps his hands behind his head and stares at the ceiling for half a minute. "Rodell Smith. He was my backup. I was supposed to be a junkie. Nichols is a big loud asshole."

"That's him."

"He didn't have any two kilos of crack, but neither did we have 50 grand. One of our so-called informants told us that Sam was dealing big-time. So we threw out the promise of $50,000. Sam, thinking we were a couple of losers, gives us about half a kilo—but it was good stuff."

"The case got dismissed?"

He frowns, stands up and walks to the window, staring at a train rumbling by. "I just don't remember. There was no search to be tossed out by a judge on the take."

"No judge ever saw the case. The state dismissed the case."

He turns around. "That almost never happens."

"The file also has been disappeared."

"Gone?"

"Yes. DELETED is all that comes up on the screen."

"You've got to be kidding!"

"That's right."

He sits, smiles and shakes his head. "I remember now. BADD took over the case."

"Bad?"

"You know: Byron Against Drug Dealers, BADD."

BADD was, is, Attorney General Herman Byron's public relations gimmick to prove that he's against drug dealers. Byron reportedly wants to be the next governor or senator. And he's a master at issuing press releases to prove his mettle for higher office. BADD was a press release, but more. It's a unit of investigators and lawyers supposed to target dealers who sell drugs to suburban kids, particularly suburban kids whose parents are white conservative voters. The State's Attorney normally is the criminal prosecutor in the county. But under legislation that Byron championed, the Attorney General can take over certain drug cases if he can demonstrate a conspiracy to sell drugs to children.

Every few months, usually on a slow news day, Byron has a press conference during which he passionately denounces drugs and drug dealers, and then announces that BADD has apprehended yet another kingpin making hundreds of millions of dollars dealing marijuana to eighth-graders. Every arrestee that I've been aware of has been a low-level street hustler/user a year or two removed from high school.

"Yeah, strange case. BADD took it over, but no press conference. A month or so later their lawyers dismissed the case. I asked the assistant AG why, and all I got was gobbledygook and legal bullshit."

"You don't think..."

"What else?" he says.

"Informants are generally low-life druggies, but Sam Nichols...I don't think he could keep his mouth shut for ten seconds."

"In which case he'd be dead by now; so maybe some kid just out of law school spent too much time reading cases and decided to cut poor Sam loose."

"Could be; but Sam Nichols had between one and three arrests every two years since he was 17. Since you collared him he's been arrest-free."

"Sounds suspicious," he says.

"You know anyone in BADD I can talk to?"

"You kidding? They're all pols or creeps or both, especially the guy who runs it, Bob the Hammer."

Bob Hamilton, or "The Hammer" as he and his press agents refer to himself, has a background in law enforcement that consists of a few years with the sheriff's police working in the southern suburbs. He was one of the few high-ranking sheriff's police officers not indicted for taking bribes from strip clubs and whorehouses about four or five years ago. Ultimately he left the force and moved over to the AG's office to run the BADD unit.

Margaret Greenspan engulfs a Victorian loveseat. She chatters on about her charges, her life and other small talk that I ignore. I met Margaret when I worked Vice. She runs an orphanage—child care facility, she'd say—for younger kids. An older man came by on a regular basis and exposed himself to the children. Apprehending the poor soul wasn't rocket science.

The skinny model magazines would never classify Margaret as beautiful or pretty. Maybe not even plain. She's short of stature, wide of girth and long past her physical prime. But she loves her job, sacrifices time and health for her kids. She laughs and smiles frequently, bantering with little boys and girls roaming in and out of the room. One little girl hops up beside her on the couch and Greenspan absentmindedly throws her arm around her, hugging her. Greenspan is one beautiful person.

I tell her about Howard Pore's death, his concern with his daughter's death and the involvement of Sam Nichols and Lilly Higgins with Community Bound. I finish, "I'm only investigating Mr. Pore's death. Other detectives are investigating the death of his daughter, Precious. However, since Pore complained about the Community Bound program and since Nichols is a suspect with respect to Mr. Pore's death..."

Greenspan laughs heartily. "Be honest: You're really dying to find out how Precious Pore got it, and why CFS set the mom and her boyfriend up in a Community Bound program. But you're getting all kinds of heat."

"You've lived in Chicago a long time," I say.

"I've labored in the Cook County vineyard for my entire adult life. There is never a shortage of...well, maybe evil is too harsh a word. Let's just say corruption. On the other hand, corruption is too decent a word. Is depravity more like it?"

"What can you tell me about Community Bound?"

"Members of my profession—and I don't exclude myself— occasionally get a bit overly optimistic about which people we can salvage. When we err, innocent children suffer."

"How would Community Bound work for Lilly and Sam?"

"They'd get intensive services: one-on-one social work, money for food, transportation, drug rehab, homemakers..."

"Homemakers?"

"Someone to help the parents get on their feet. Cooks, cleans, supposed to demonstrate to the parent how to take care of a home. This person is not a social worker, but a nonprofessional working

103

under one. Four or five private agencies contract with CFS to provide homemakers." Greenspan, one of those people who find humor even in the bleakest of situations, suddenly turns serious. "Leaving aside politics, even murder, this is a very serious case of apparent child abuse. Vaginal tears and burns do not add up to Community Bound. They add up to Juvenile Court and temporary custody for the older child. Where did you say she is?"

"Don't know."

"There are three child ecology units in the area—but the death occurred two months ago?"

"Right."

"A child would normally be on such a unit for about a week." She walks over to a desk, sits and pulls the phone toward her. "The unit is staffed by generally a psychiatrist, several pediatricians, psychologists and social workers with an expertise in testing young children. This is essential for sex abuse cases involving very young children." She turns back to the phone and spends the next several minutes talking on it. After finishing the last phone call, she comes back to the couch. "Asha Pore wasn't in any of the three units during the past six months."

"How did you get that information?"

"You heard. I called and asked."

"What about all this 'confidentiality' that everyone keeps throwing at me?"

"Confidentiality," she laughs, "is to prevent the public from knowing about our victories. We know that the public at large will consider our philosophy just a little goofy, so we keep them away from it. Precious Pore's death was not a failure from the point of view of the system. It was a success. The patient just happened to die."

"Since you seem to be able to open some doors, maybe you can open a few for me."

"Oh boy, here it comes."

"Find out if Lilly and Sam had a home care worker, and if they did, her name."

"I'll try..."

104

As I stand, my pager beeps. I phone and get Jeanette Pore. "I be gettin' a big runaround here at Juvenile Court. Can you help, Miss?" I had told Jeanette to file a petition because I felt that if she actually got in front of the judge, he might say something to reveal why he opted for Community Bound. Of course, I realized that he'd probably deny her request. My guilt and the fact that the court is 15 minutes away prompt me to meet her.

Four-and-a-half hours' sleep, too much running around and the memory of Sam's paws on my behind overwhelm me. I put my head on the steering wheel, close my eyes and unwillingly doze off for a minute or two before my cell phone jars me back to a murky reality. "You okay?" Jeff asks.

"Sure, why?"

"You sound groggy."

"I am."

"You can't keep working these hours. It'll kill you."

"Just this case. It'll go away."

"It's not the case. You haven't been yourself."

"Just the case."

"You need time out. I talked to the kid next door. She can babysit tonight. Let's go out, have a quiet dinner, a bottle of wine."

"That's sweet of you, Jeffrey, but I'd crash after smelling the wine. Maybe over the weekend."

"You by yourself?"

"Unfortunately."

"Be careful. And Carol..."

"Yes?"

"I love you."

So many answers come into my head. I manage, "I know that, Jeff."

CHAPTER 7

"Sorry to be a bother, Miss."

"You're no bother, and my name is Carol."

"These folks in the clerk's office are mighty ignorant. Won't give a person the time of day."

"I'll try it. And for now I'm not a cop." That is, I think, if I don't want to be guarding the morgue on the midnight shift.

"You a lawyer?" a bored-looking, heavyset middle-aged black woman in a yellow smock sporting the insignia of the Clerk of the Circuit Court of Cook County asks.

"No."

"CFS social worker?"

"No."

"Then I can't help you."

"Why?"

"These files are secret."

"We don't need to see the file. Ms. Pore wants to set the case on Judge Roostman's docket."

"She a lawyer? The lady asks pointing to Jeanette."

"No."

"She the parent?"

"No. She's the children's grandmother."

"Lady, you're not telling me anything this here lady already ain't told me, and it don't make no difference to me that you're some kind of smart muckety-muck. You're not nothin' as far as I'm concerned, and neither is she."

Jeanette looks at me expecting some kind of middle-class action in the face of such vile bureaucratic ignorance. But falling back on my badge could banish me to the morgue. I beat a momentary retreat.

"Why not tell that fat ass that you're a cop and that's the way it is?"

"It's a bit more complicated," I say as we walk to Roostman's courtroom.

After about 15 minutes, the lead Public Defender emerges from the courtroom. He sees me and immediately scurries back in. I flash my badge to the bailiff and he accommodatingly opens the door for me. The courtroom is relatively small, at least by Criminal Court standards. The judge sits on a slightly elevated bench. He is a good-looking, middle-aged black man with hair groomed naturally and cut short. A half-dozen young professional types stand in front of him discussing something or other. Standing slightly behind them are three females: one about 45, one about 19 and one about three. Three tables face the bench, at which younger professional types sit scrawling on yellow pads or reading official-looking documents. A few social-work types sit on the two benches in the rear. The chief PD occupies a chair at one of the tables with his head buried three inches from a file that he pretends to read. I poke him on the shoulders.

"You don't belong here," he whispers.

"The bailiff doesn't agree."

"Probably thought you're involved in a case."

"I am."

"Not any case here."

"Let's talk."

"I like my job."

The judge looks up as our whispering gets louder. He doesn't say anything, but gives us one of those judge looks. The PD stands and I follow him out of the courtroom. He hustles me into a small conference room.

"Detective Moore, I like what I do."

"Great. So do I. So we'll keep this little meeting a mutual secret."

"You can't see our file."

"I need advice." I tell him about our encounter in the clerk's office.

"I can't be visible in this case," he says, "but march back in there and ask for Form 725a. It's an emergency motion. Fill it out. The clerk must put it on the judge's two o'clock docket for tomorrow."

"That's all?"

"Yeah. But you better have a real emergency or he'll toss you out of the courtroom in ten seconds, even sanction you. And with this case, you'd better have a lawyer like the president of the Bar Association."

Jeanette and I tramp back to the same clerk sitting behind the same desk and smirking with the same smug arrogance. "Whatchya want now?"

"Form 725a."

"Can't have it."

"We'll talk to your supervisor."

The arrogance remains. The smugness is replaced with hatred. She throws a triplicate form at us. I fill it out, claiming that the emergency is because of Jeanette's inability to visit Asha and vice versa.

The clerk stamps it and throws us a copy. "This ain't no emergency."

"You the judge?"

"No, bitch, but I know the clerk in Roostman's court and I'm gonna talk to him and he'll mention it to the judge. Maybe you'll get yourself tossed in jail for perjury."

"What do you think?" Jeanette asks as we exit the building.

"Maybe best to forget it."

"And let those fools push me around? Not after what happened to my boy. Can you help?"

"Don't think so."

"Do I get a Public Defender?"

"No. That's only for the people who are in jeopardy, parents."

"I can't pay for no lawyer. But I'll do my best."

"The judge probably won't let you talk," I say.

"Maybe Legal Aid."

"Not on 24 hours' notice. Let me see what I can do." I think about Andrew's law firm and all those young lawyers pushing papers who might love to see the inside of a real courtroom.

I check my pager and, among other callers, Andrew has left a message. I call him, but he's at a deposition. I say that I'm returning his call—a good excuse, since I'm really calling him to see if I can pry one of his young lawyers loose. Margaret Greenspan also called. I phone her. "Theresa Caedman."

"What?"

"Your homemaker."

"You work quick."

"You'd better, too. The person I got the name from was suspicious. You never know who she might talk to."

Theresa Caedman lives in one of the thousands of brick bungalows built shortly after the first World War that fill up much of Chicago's South Side. In fact, once inside, it reminds me of the one I grew up in: a small living room, a smaller, dark dining room, one bedroom off the living room and two off the dining room. A small kitchen and a back room are in the rear and, like many other similar bungalows, some owner over the years had renovated the attic into extra living space.

Theresa is a little shorter than myself and very thin. Unlike many African-Americans when confronted with a police officer, she is not a bit guarded. She introduces me to an adolescent boy and girl, and then herds them out of the living room as we sit down. Pictures of the two kids and of a middle-aged man in a bus driver's uniform grace the top of the television.

"A female police detective! I'm impressed. Keisha, that's my junior in high school, says she wants to major in Criminal Justice in college—though I don't know how we can afford it. She wants to be a police detective, Homicide. Can you imagine? But you're a Homicide detective. Keisha, come back in here, girl!"

The thin, pretty girl who resembles her mother comes back in and politely but shyly puts up with her mother asking me questions about my police career and educational background. I give her an abridged, even romantic version, leaving out encounters like the one with Sam. After five or six minutes, I try to regain the advantage and redirect the conversation. "But Mrs. Caedman, I'm here to question you."

She laughs. "And so you are. Keisha, go do your homework so you can sit here in about 15 years with a star yourself. And tell Bobby to get away from that Nintendo and get to his books. Now, sweetie, how can I help you?"

I prod her with a number of questions. As I ask the first, tears well up in her eyes. "My two little angels," she sighs. "And Precious may have the better part of it, except for the way she died." She puts her head down and brings out a tissue. "Those two, Sam and Lilly, are poor excuses for human beings. The one's a flake and the other's a...God forgive me, but I can't think of a word evil enough to describe him. He's pure evil, and a racist too. Can't tell you the number of times he referred to the kids as niggers. Me too. Once.

"No ma'am, those kids should never have been left home with Sam and Lilly. And I'd be there just three times a week for four hours. I was supposed to work with Lilly—show her how to keep the place clean, how to make decent food for the kids. But she spent her days laying around half-naked smoking reefer and drinking Bloody Marys. Instead of working with her, I ended up doing it all myself—not for her or Sam, but for those babies.

"I'd get in about 10:30. On most days Sam and Lilly would be in bed while Asha is watching TV, and Precious in her crib screaming and soaked right through to the skin with her booty red as a Santa Claus suit. Sam would sometimes sleep until one or two in the afternoon.

"You kidding? I told those two social workers about Sam and Lilly. Put it in my reports. They ignored me. Said I should do my job, they'd do theirs. You know how social workers are. They know everything. I know nothing.

"They were there maybe four, five times when I was there, and once they got into an argument with Lilly and Sam. Except, you know, social workers don't argue. They raise issues, talk about feelings—reasonable, quiet, soothing.

"Lilly and Sam were supposed to do drug drops every few weeks. I don't think they ever went. Joslin told them they had to go. Sam went off on her. Told her to F-off. Joslin said Lilly could be losing her children. Lilly starts screaming and Sam told her to go see Clarence.

"I'm not too sure who Clarence is, but I'm thinking he's a tall, dignified-looking white fellow who came by the house once.

Didn't actually come up. I heard Sam tell Lilly he's gonna see Clarence downstairs. I looked out the window—not that I'm nosy, mind you—and saw this very tall man with slicked-back brown hair, and I'm sure he wore glasses. They were talking down there maybe ten minutes, and this tall fella drove away. Afterwards Sam came up and was real sullen-like. Heard him telling Lilly he was gonna get himself killed.

"She just said he could go to jail instead. She was always making sarcastic remarks like that. Half the time Sam would push her. The other half he'd just grunt. This time he said he was gonna get laid by a real woman and left out.

"Yeah, Sam was usually high on crack, drugs, beer or vodka. And he always had money.

"I never went back after Precious died. They took Asha out of the home, wouldn't tell me where. But according to the grapevine, it's the Mom and kids' shelter, 'cause that's where Joslin and Pearson have their office. They want to be real near her. You want my opinion? They goofed big-time, and now they're out to cover up.

"Sure, they talked to me, and gave me all the confidentiality BS. Told me I'd go to jail if I talked to anyone." She laughs. "You're not anyone. You be the man." She gets serious. "Keep my name out of it, sweetie. I need the job if Keisha's gonna get through college and be a Homicide detective."

It's past seven o'clock, dusk and long past the time when I should be home, or at least phone home. I dial Jeffrey. He sounds subdued, almost distracted. "We've eaten. I figured you'd be late, and yeah, the kids are doing fine, and no, they've had no junk food, and yes, I'm seeing a divorce lawyer tomorrow, and..."

"I was the drama student."

"Oh yes, I remember you now. We got married, didn't we?"

"For better or worse."

"Does that include absent?"

"Didn't you just a few hours ago tell me you loved me?"

"And that's why I want to see you. I love you. I want to be near you."

"What's gotten into you?"

"No, Carol...what's gotten into you?"

"Work. Professionalism. And, my dear husband, money for our mortgage, car payments..."

"We share the bills. What about ourselves?"

"I don't want to discuss our relationship over a cell phone."

"That's the only time we're not too tired to do it."

"You're being a bit dramatic. I was home all last week."

"If you were gone a few nights, okay. That's not the future I see. And let's just cut to the chase. You've been drawing away, almost cold. You're just not the same person."

"We've made love twice in the past several days."

"We've had sex."

"What are you saying?"

"I don't know. You're different. I suppose it's the job. I hope it's the job."

I have no response—no honest response. Besides, as dusk gives way to night, I stare over the hood of the car at the string of bungalows, barely discernible, and think maybe Jeffrey is right—even though, gratefully, he doesn't have all the facts. And perhaps I still love him as deeply as before. But he's become hopelessly mixed in with the poison that has almost imperceptibly seeped into my soul: the druggies, con men, pimps, whores, wife-batterers, child abusers, sex perverts, drunks; and now the corpses and killers, not to mention bored, burnt-out and macho cops, along with the decent Tommy Welch, Ollie Tate and Ronny Ramirez types. Maybe I hate Jeff because he is an integral part of my life and I detest my life right now? And perhaps Andrew is just an illusion of love, an escape from the poison.

"Carol?"

"Huh?"

"What's wrong?"

"Nothing."

"You're not saying anything."

"I'm okay. I've got to work late again."

"Jesus."

"It won't go on. I promise you."

"You mean the job or our marriage?"

"Jeffrey."

113

"Just being facetious. Love you. Love you a lot."

"Me too," I say, disconnect and phone Andrew, for once feeling not guilty. This call is business.

Two hours later, after dining at Wendy's and walking aimlessly up and down Michigan Avenue, I sit on Andrew's couch, letting the tip of my tongue touch but not sip his wine. He sits on the couch, facing me with his knee propped up on the cushion separating us. The ceiling lights are out. A small antique Tiffany lamp shoots out tiny shimmers of soft green light about the room. The door is locked.

He leans forward and kisses me softly on the lips. I respond and caress the back of his head and neck. And as I respond I feel almost nauseated by the instinctiveness of my reactions: how comfortable I am with Andrew, and how devastating that comfort level could become to my family. I pull away.

"Christ, you're one bizarre contradiction." He leans forward and kisses my legs, which pushes my skirt up even higher. His head bounces back up. "I love the taste of nylon."

My ambivalence evaporates. I put the glass down and grab the back of his hair, pushing myself on top of him and shoving my tongue into his mouth. I prop myself up on his chest. "Of course, we can't do anything here."

"This is not anything?"

"This is a very confused woman."

"I'm not confused. At least about my feelings. I've never been near a more exciting, more desirable woman. Christ, I need you."

I pull myself off him and sit up. "I'm really sorry about all this. I'm here to talk business."

"This is the only business I can think of right now."

I put my finger on his lips. "Deferred gratification. For now I need your wisdom."

"Shoot!" He kisses my shoulder and fondles my breast.

I remove his hands. "I can't concentrate."

"I'm listening," he says licking my shoulder, "but give me the end of the story first."

"What do you mean?"

"What do you want?"

"A *pro bono* lawyer."

"For whom, where and when?"

"For the mother of the man whose murder I'm investigating, at Juvenile Court, tomorrow."

He leans back. "Even if I wanted to help, I can't. Free legal work must go through the firm's *pro bono* committee –- which, coincidentally, I'm on. But a draft outlining the case and just why we should get involved must be submitted at least two weeks prior to our once-a-month meeting. Normally, we only take appeals or criminal or constitutional cases. We've never gone to Juvenile Court. But tell me about the case." He feigns an interest that I know isn't there—particularly since he returns immediately to kissing my neck and shoulders and fondling my breasts.

I give the abbreviated version: how Howard's murder led me to his mother, which led me to visit Lilly and Sam, Pearson and Joslin, Flynn and Albert and the State's Attorney Lenore Weurster, which prompted Captain Robertson to come down hard on me, which led me to Tommy Welch, my visits with Karen Hanson and Ronny Ramirez, what I learned from Margaret Greenspan and finally why getting Jeanette Pore in front of Judge Roostman could be helpful to the investigation.

While I speak, Andrew's lips play on my shoulders. His fingers nimbly unbutton my blouse. The story becomes increasingly incoherent, while I get increasingly turned on. When I finish, I turn and embrace him. For once he seems disinterested. He leans back, clasps his hands behind his head and stares at the ceiling. "The judge will toss Grandma's motion out in five seconds, ruling that she has no standing even to argue for such visits. You say that this fellow Sam had a serious drug case dismissed by the Attorney General. You think he might be an informant for BADD, and they used their influence to protect him and his girlfriend?"

"Speculation. It could have just as well have been all the social workers."

"Sam's ex-wife told you that federal narcotics agents came down hard on her, but a short while later two FBI agents told her that Sam was cool."

"That's right, but..."

Andrew stands up and tucks his shirt in while walking to the large ceiling-to-floor windows overlooking the city. "Sam dealt with someone named Clarence. What did he look like?"

"Tall, glasses."

"Like the FBI agent who visited Karen?"

"Yes."

"Clarence Johnson."

"What?"

"Clarence Johnson is the chief of the Bureau's government corruption unit. Something's way out of kilter here. Why would the Feds be interested in Sam Nichols?" he asks the window and the city. "Now, if Joan Tatle was involved, we'd have ourselves a bullseye."

I stand, straightening out my clothes. "What was that name?"

"Joan Tatle is out of the Justice Department, Washington. She's assigned to the Chicago office to handle all major corruption cases in the Midwest and South. You don't recognize the name?"

"No."

"Interesting stuff you've stumbled on."   He smiles.

"I'd better get going."

"Stay."

"No.

"When will I see you again?"

"We need breathing room."

He looks hurt. "I want to be naked with you."

"Maybe. We'll see." I gently push him away and pick up my purse. Suddenly I remember Albert and Flynn's report. "Come to think of it, the Homicide reports by the two detectives, Flynn and Albert, stated that a J.R.T. phoned them several times about the case."

He spins, darts to a shelf on the wall behind his desk and pulls down an orange book, the Chicago Legal Directory. He pages through it and then announces, "Joan Russit Tatle—J.R.T. Bullseye! Bullseye and bullseye again! Detective Moore, you have hit the major, major leagues."

"I don't understand."

"Neither do I, not yet; but a picture is definitely emerging. It's murky, but I can see the outlines." He walks back to the window

116

and stares at the night for several minutes before speaking again. "It just might work."

"What are you talking about?"

He turns toward me. "Do you know the caption of the case?"

"Which case?"

"The case where your Granny needs representation."

"Well, yes, I have a copy of her motion." I give it to him.

He stares at the one-page document for several seconds and smiles. "Yes, it may work." He picks up the phone. "Dennis, get down here. Now!"

Less than two minutes later, a tall, thin young man in his late twenties arrives. He stands at attention in front of Andrew. "What are you working on, Dennis?"

"The Goldberg papers."

"Drop it."

"They're due next week."

"We'll just have to work harder over the weekend. I need a memorandum of law on my desk no later than tomorrow morning. Here's the caption. Keep the facts simple and brief. The judge is prejudiced against the petitioner because he permitted a child to return to her parents, knowing that the parents were neglectful and potentially abusive and that the child would be vulnerable. Because of this, the court will be defensive and not give the petitioner a fair hearing on her motion to have visits with her grandchild.

"You won't find any case on point; but load the memo up with lots of case law, preferably from the US and Illinois Supreme Courts. I recall an article in last year's *DePaul Law Review* on under what circumstances a change of venue will be granted. Pull that out and throw in a lot of that language as well. The bottom line has to be that once we make the allegation, the judge is compelled to refer the matter to another judge for a determination of whether the first judge is prejudiced or not. Make that statement at the beginning, middle and end.

"And you'll find a line of cases holding that lawyers who make frivolous claims of a judge's prejudice can be sanctioned by way of large fines. Put in a section including those cases to show the judge that we are aware of the consequences of filing the motion."

"It'll be on your desk tomorrow morning."

"Not good enough. Six o'clock. Good. Shut the door behind you."

"So?" I ask.

Andrew fumbles with some papers. "So what?"

"What about the *pro bono* committee?"

"They won't be involved."

"What do you mean?"

"I'll personally handle the case."

"Won't someone around here complain?"

"Let them. I'll need your help, of course."

"I'll never get permission."

"You don't need it. We'll drop a subpoena on you tomorrow morning. You'll have to be in court."

"Robertson and the rest of the brass will see right through that."

"There's clout on the other side of this case, but we're about to bring some in on your side now. I can handle the likes of Robertson. The question is whether I can handle the likes of whoever is really pulling the strings behind this case. And that's what makes this whole mess interesting."

On the way home I try to soothe the butterflies fluttering about in my stomach as I plan how to deal with the confrontation that will surely occur with Jeffrey. But I find him in the living room, reading a book and sipping a beer. He offers to heat up dinner. I decline and pour myself a glass of wine. He asks me about the case. I tell him about Margaret Greenspan and Theresa Caedman and leave Andrew out. I ask him about his day. He tells me about classes, students, dinner and the now-sleeping kids. I feign an interest, but he senses the truth. "I'm tired," he says, kisses me and goes upstairs, leaving me with my wine and reverie.

CHAPTER 8

I get to the office by eight in the morning. Andrew is on my voicemail as of midnight, asking me to call him as soon as I get in.

"Great. Thanks for calling. No, take that side out. It cuts against our case. And move that paragraph to the end. And..."

"What are you talking about?"

"Sorry, I'm going over our briefs. Just start on it. I'll catch you later."

"What?"

"Sorry, Carol. Got much to finish before 1:30. But in my haste to get going, I never did get my client's name and phone number. Could you bring her down?"

I give him the essentials of Jeanette Pore. "But I'd rather stay low-profile."

"I understand. But fill her in. We'll follow up and bring her in. See you at 1:30."

"Andrew?" But he's gone.

I phone Jeanette, who knows nothing about Andrew. She certainly would not understand how his firm won't touch a case for less than a $25,000 retainer. But she is ecstatic knowing that she'll walk into court with a real lawyer. Later I receive a subpoena, and pursuant to department regulations, I notify Sergeant Malone. "Kinda late to get paper to be in court in the afternoon," he says. "Should we get the state to quash it?"

"It's on the Pore case. I'd be there anyway, just to see what's going down."

"Watch your step. You don't need Robertson and his pals blowing smoke up your...behind."

Of course I don't. Worse, I'm beginning to worry about Andrew's judgment. I'd like to see him a bit more deliberative. Nevertheless, at 1:30, I'm outside Roostman's courtroom. Neither Andrew nor Jeanette is there, but Lenore Weurster is. "What brings you here, Detective Sweetie?" she asks.

"The contemplative atmosphere."

"A smartass."

I hand her my subpoena.

"This was issued this morning," she says. "We'll get the judge to quash it."

"That's between you and the judge."

"You've been around long enough to know that you could have called and we'd have done it without your presence."

"I just follow the law."

"It's not because the person issuing the subpoena happens to be one of the biggest names in the legal field? Or for that matter, because he's Mr. Hollywood?"

"What did you tell me the other day? Shake your boobs, wiggle your buns..." I walk away.

"Wait a second," Weurster says, grasping my arm. "You work for us—which means you work with us."

"Ms. Weurster, I work for the people of the city of Chicago."

"And I work for the taxpayers too, so we'll work together."

"At arriving at truth and justice."

"I don't like you."

Over Weurster's shoulder I see Andrew and Jeanette Pore walking toward us. I quickly move away from Weurster, hoping that Andrew and Jeanette will not greet me. Andrew walks by as if I'm invisible.

Not Jeanette Pore: She throws her arms around me. "Thank you so much. I..." I give her a meaningful look and she stops in mid-sentence.

"Mrs. Pore, I'm Lenore Weurster, an Assistant State's Attorney. I'm sorry about your son's death."

Andrew is immediately at Jeanette's side. "You are..."

"Lenore Weurster, Deputy Chief State's Attorney. I'm in charge of the Juvenile Court office."

"Who's handling this particular case?" Andrew asks as they shake hands.

"I am."

"This is a petty matter for someone of your rank," Andrew says.

"And ditto for you," Weurster says.

"Are you in favor of visits?"

"I don't think that Ms. Pore should be permitted to intervene as a party. After all, this case is about alleged parental child neglect. The grandparents are not parties."

"But surely you won't object to us getting into the case for the sole purpose of the visits?"

"I may, if we decide that the visits are inappropriate. I understand that the mother is opposed to visits. I haven't spoken with the workers."

"You oppose intervention?"

"Mr. Malcolm, I want to help Mrs. Pore. I suggest putting the case over for 30 days; and all things being equal, at that point we may be in favor of some kind of supervised visits."

"Thank you, Ms. Weurster, but we're not interested."

"We'll see you in court then, Mr. Malcolm." Weurster turns and disappears into the courtroom.

Andrew holds out his hand. "Detective Moore," acting for all the world like he doesn't know me. I take his hand and nod professionally.

Several minutes later the bailiff barks out that our case is ready and ushers us into the courtroom. A court reporter sits below and to one side of the judge. A clerk is on the other. We stand in front of the bench.

"Please identify yourselves for the record," Judge Roostman says crisply. Andrew, Weurster, Jeanette and I state our names.

"What's the nature of this case?" Roostman asks, seemingly confused.

"Your Honor, Ms. Pore filed a motion yesterday seeking visits with her granddaughter," Andrew says.

"That seems reasonable," Roostman says. "Any objections?"

"Yes, Your Honor," Weurster says.

"State them."

121

"Judge, Ms. Pore is not a party to this proceeding and has no legal standing to file a motion."

"Mr. Malcolm?"

"I have anticipated this and prepared a memorandum of law on the issue of standing. Every Illinois Supreme Court case has held that relative intervention is up to the discretion of the court, and that the court must be guided by what is in the child's best interest."

"Of course I haven't seen Mr. Malcolm's brief. And I have no objection to his filing it. But the state would ask for 30 days to respond," Weurster says.

"Judge, if we can prepare a memorandum of law in one night, surely the state can..."

Roostman cuts Andrew off. "Ms. Weurster, there will be no need for a memorandum. This matter is discretionary with the court, and I will permit Ms. Pore to intervene as a party to seek visits with her grandchild. What is your position with respect to that issue?"

"I need a week to discuss it with the DCFS workers."

Roostman leafs through a very thin file. "Frankly, I do not recall this case; but denying a grandmother visits would be quite unusual. The case certainly appears routine. The mother and her paramour were heavily involved in drugs, their apartment filthy and their young children not exactly thriving. According to the records, I kept the children home at the suggestion of Children and Family Services, who were to place them in the Community Bound program. Is all that correct?" he asks, putting down the pages from which he has been reading.

"Up to a point, Your Honor," Weurster says. "There has been an unfortunate accident and Precious, the younger daughter, has died."

"What kind of accident?"

"She apparently pulled a pan of boiling water on top of herself."

The judge shakes his head while looking at the papers in front of him. He looks up, apparently trying to remain judicious and cloak his anger. "When did this happen?"

"About eight weeks ago."

"Why wasn't the case brought back in? Why wasn't this Court informed?"

"It was an accident."

"Ms. Weurster, these children were sent home by me to two marginal people under the protection of the state's child welfare system. I am not suggesting that the accident was anything more than an accident; but accidents sometimes are caused by neglect. And isn't that why we're here? To judge neglect?"

"But that's not why we're here on this particular case at this particular moment."

"Oh yes: the question of visits. And are you alleging that Ms. Pore, the grandmother, had something to do with the accident?"

"No, Your Honor."

"Was she present?"

"No, Your Honor."

Roostman appears exasperated and turns to Andrew. "And what is your pleasure, Mr. Malcolm?"

"With all due respect to this court, I request a change of venue."

I can't believe Andrew's response. If Roostman knew anything about this case, he should be up for an Academy Award. He respects Andrew and is pissed off at Weurster for not informing him about the child's death. He's ripe not only to grant immediate visits, but even to grant a hearing as to the cause of the child's death—which would get a lot of the stuff that I'm looking for into the open.

The judge leafs through the pages of the thick documents that Andrew hands up to him. Looking like she's about to froth at the mouth, Weurster weaves back and forth from leg to leg as she skim-reads the same papers. Finally the judge looks at Andrew. "Mr. Malcolm, I have been on the bench long enough not to take this kind of matter personally. But I must say that the implications of this document are very disturbing…and I might add, insofar as this particular jurist is concerned, inaccurate."

"Again, with all due respect, that is for another judge to decide."

"I'm well aware of that, Counsel."

"But that's not true!" Weurster cries out, her voice crackling with anger. "Another judge must rule on your alleged prejudice towards Ms. Pore; but to get to that stage, Mr. Malcolm must present some limited showing of this court's bias. This document reeks of the rankest hearsay gossip and allegations that would be clearly libelous outside of the four corners of a court document."

Roostman stands. "I think that the lawyers in this case should adjourn to chambers so that we can discuss this matter rationally and off the record. Any objection?"

Weurster shrugs her shoulders in an affirmative kind of way, but Andrew speaks up. "I have no objection, as long as Detective Moore accompanies us."

"Detective Moore is not an attorney, is not involved in this particular Juvenile case, does not work for Mr. Malcolm, is not covered by the attorney/client privilege and, most importantly, is a witness subpoenaed by Mr. Malcolm, apparently to give evidence in this matter," Weurster growls.

"Mr. Malcolm?" Roostman asks.

"I subpoenaed Detective Moore because she is involved in an aspect of the case and hence has knowledge of some of the allegations in my motion. However, I won't call her as a witness if she attends the conference. Further, I am sure that Detective Moore will agree to be bound by any guidelines with respect to confidentiality set down by this court. Because of the nature of my motion, I feel the need to have an unbiased observer present at discussions held off the record."

"Off the record," Roostman almost but not quite snaps as he visibly tries to hold down his emotions. The court reporter places her hands on her machine to demonstrate that she is not typing. "Mr. Malcolm, your reputation as a litigator and preeminent member of the bar precedes you, and I presume that most of your practice is devoted to courtrooms other than in this building."

"That's correct, Your Honor."

"I can assure you that counsel here for the state as well as myself know and understand the Canons of Ethics, and no one in this courtroom will sandbag you in any off-the-record discussion."

"Judge Roostman, your reputation also precedes you as a judge of absolute integrity and fairness. However, once having set a course of action, which I have done, I must insist that a neutral observer be present in an off-the-record, in-chambers meeting. Detective Moore is employed by the people of the state and hence is an appropriate and unbiased witness."

"Let's go," the judge says abruptly and walks down to a door to the left of the bench. We follow him to his chambers. He pours himself a cup of coffee without offering any to the rest of us and flops into a big leather chair behind a small desk. The three lawyers sit in the chairs facing the desk. I sit on a couch in the rear of the compact chambers.

"Mr. Malcolm, according to your motion, I should not hear Ms. Pore's request for visitation because of my prejudice, or alleged prejudice, which results from the fact that I sent the children to reside with their mother and the mother's paramour, where one child subsequently died under suspicious circumstances." The judge glared. "The motion implies—though never really claims—that I knew that I was sending the child into a dangerous situation, but that I did so for political reasons that I knew or should have known about. You then allege that after Precious' death, the case involving the second child, Asha, was not brought before this court because of a continued conspiracy between public officials—of whom I may be one—and the parents of the child. Mr. Malcolm, if your reputation were not so well entrenched, I'd assume that these allegations were the ravings of a paranoid madman."

"Your Honor, I am prepared to present testimony concerning the inferences that you draw from my motion."

Roostman throws back his head and laughs. "As if these 'inferences' aren't what any reasonably intelligent person would draw. But you give yourself room, so that if you fail to prove these charges—I mean 'inferences'—you won't get sanctioned."

Andrew remains unflustered. "I represent a client, Jeanette Pore."

Roostman leans forward, his arms firmly planted on the desk. "And that's the real issue here, I presume. Not the allegations, assertions, inferences, implications or whatever you want to call them. You want visits between Ms. Pore and her grandchild. Right?"

"That's correct. But..."

"No, Mr. Malcolm, that is the nub of what you request. I gave you the right to intervene solely for that issue, correct?"

"You are quite correct."

"So if that happens, you have no other complaint, at least with this court?"

"Correct."

The judge turns to Weurster. "Why can't you permit Ms. Pore to visit her granddaughter? That lady out there doesn't strike me as an axe murderer."

"I'll take up the matter with the social workers. The child is quite upset."

"So much the better to visit with a familiar face, someone who loves her. In the ordinary course of events, grannies are great nurturers."

"Judge, this is not an ordinary case."

"That's what Mr. Malcolm has been telling me, and I've been telling him that he's paranoid. Am I to take it that he's not?"

"Mr. Malcolm knows nothing about this case, except perhaps what Detective Moore has been feeding him, and she's a new detective with no experience..."

"I resent this attack on a Chicago police officer by an Assistant State's..."

Roostman cuts him off. "You're quite right, Mr. Malcolm. Ms. Weurster, we are here to cut through the crap and hopefully arrive at substantial justice. We are not here to attack each other or anyone else."

Weurster quietly but unrepentantly proceeds. "The child did not live with her father, who was Ms. Pore's son. I understand that relations between the child's mother and Ms. Pore are rather strained. There are differences."

"Aside from race?" Roostman asks sarcastically.

"Well, uh, yes. The mother, Lilly Higgins, and her paramour, Sam Nichols, just do not get along with Ms. Pore."

"Ms. Weurster, you're jabbering in circles. This case came in because the child's mother, Ms. Higgins, and the mother's paramour were fairly reprehensible parents. They were heavy drug users, lived in a filthy apartment, had little food and often left the two kids alone to fend for themselves."

"Well, er, yes."

"And the Department of Children and Family Services' job, according to what your office apparently asked of me when the case appeared here—what I assume you asked of me, because I cannot recall anything about this—was to take control of the

126

situation, provide services to the parents, supervise them and make sure the children were well taken care of and protected. In that case, the Department failed."

"It was an accident."

"We'll get to that in a moment. The Department failed, insofar as the child died either by design, by neglect or perhaps just by a plain old unavoidable accident. But part of protecting a child is assuring that concerned relatives are hooked up with the kid— particularly in a case where the parents are, well, less than model parents. But what I see here is a specific plan to put roadblocks between the child and a person who seems to be a very concerned grandparent. At least she was concerned enough to go out and get one of the finest and most expensive lawyers in Chicago—whom I presume she cannot afford to pay."

"In the first place, I doubt that Ms. Pore obtained the services of Mr. Malcolm without the help of...well, never mind. But you are being unfair to the Department, whose only charge is to do what is in a child's best interest, not to facilitate bonding with grandparents."

"But in a case like this, bonding with the Grandma would definitely seem to be in the kid's best interest."

"Maybe you're right. Maybe not. I would like to confer with the experts, the workers," Weurster says.

"What about supervised visits in the meantime?"

"Very tightly supervised is within the realm of possibility."

"You mean that if Ms. Pore and the child discuss embarrassing issues, like her sister's death, you would terminate the visits?" Andrew asks.

"I mean that the workers would terminate visits if they felt that the visit was upsetting to the child."

"So their subjective judgment rules," Andrew says.

"They are the experts."

"Let's get back to this accident," Roostman says. "Why the hell wasn't that information, with a detailed investigation of the circumstances surrounding this child's death, brought before me?"

"We and the Department investigated and determined that the death was a horrible accident. But the child's death is irrelevant to this motion."

"Ms. Weurster, it is not irrelevant to me. I signed an order sending the children back home under the Department's supervision. One died, scalded to death. I can presume, hope, that this was not a homicide; but it certainly could well be neglect. Most parents don't leave pots of boiling water on a stove where a toddler can pull it on top of herself."

"The Department thought otherwise."

"I am the judge. I have the final authority on the case. It is my responsibility—my decision, not the social workers'—to determine abuse and neglect."

"They are the experts."

"Then let them wear these robes. They are perhaps witnesses. I am the judge. And Ms. Weurster, at some point—soon, I presume— you will bring that case before me."

"You can bet your life on that, Judge."

"Mr. Malcolm, are you satisfied with supervised visits until Ms. Weurster reports about unsupervised visits?"

"About how long would that take?"

"Thirty to 40 days," Weurster says.

"Not interested."

"What about two weeks?" Roustman asks.

"We can't do that, Judge," Weurster says.

"And I'm not interested in two weeks. We'll take the supervised visits for a few days, but we want to get the unsupervised visits as quickly as possible."

"And a change of venue, which between a hearing on the motion for a change and the actual motion for visits could take several weeks or more. In the meantime, your client won't have any visits, supervised or otherwise," Roostman replies.

"I understand the implications of my request."

"Well, Mr. Malcolm, Ms. Weurster is quite correct. Before I refer the matter to another judge for a hearing to determine if I am prejudiced, I must be convinced that you have presented at least some kind of showing on the face of your complaint, either by testimony or affidavit, that there is some merit to your allegations."

"That is unduly burdensome, since I will have to turn around and use the same witnesses before a second judge showing prejudice. What you, in fact, want is for me to present two hearings."

"Appeal me."

"So it will take me six months to a year to get relief."

"You filed the motion. You are an experienced lawyer and advise me that you have reasons for your course of action. You will show me your *prima facie* case at two p.m. tomorrow. Will you be ready, Ms. Weurster?"

"Of course. We have no witnesses."

Andrew leans back, straightens his tie, pulls on his cuffs and calmly says, "I have a problem with tomorrow's date and the state has another."

"We can take care of ourselves, Mr. Malcolm, and I can assure you that we have no problems," Weurster says.

"What's up?" Roostman asks.

"In the first place, all our witnesses are hostile, so we must subpoena them. I can do that, but we'll require at least an additional 24 hours. Secondly, Ms. Weurster is one of those hostile witnesses that I plan to call."

Weurster slams a yellow pad on Roustman's desk. "This is the biggest pile of horseshit that I've ever seen. I am the attorney in this case and have attorney/client and work product privileges. Even if I know something, he can't call me to testify."

Roostman smiles. "That's not correct, of course, Ms. Weurster, as I'm sure you'll recognize in a more rational moment. Mr. Malcolm can call you and ask any question he wants. It's up to me to judge whether the questions involve privilege or relevant material—after, of course, a proper objection. If Mr. Malcolm persists in calling you, you'll have to assign another assistant to handle at least this aspect of the case."

He looks at Andrew. "Do you have any other bombshell witnesses?"

"I'm more than happy to give you and Ms. Weurster the names of those whom I hope to call."

"That's very gracious of you," Weurster says sarcastically.

Roostman leans back and swivels around while folding his hands together as if in prayer. "Please, Mr. Malcolm, so advise us."

"Aside from Ms. Weurster, we intend to call Detectives Flynn and Albert, who allegedly investigated the death of Precious Pore.

129

We also will be seeking their entire investigative file. We will also call the two DCFS workers, Jena Joslin and Patty Pearson. Besides them, we'll need Sam Nichols, Special Agent Clarence Williams of the FBI and Assistant United States Attorney Joan Tatle. We will be seeking the US Attorney's file on Mr. Nichols as well."

Roostman grins a big toothy smile. "Mr. Malcolm, either you are one smart, tough cookie with enormous brass balls, or you're one stupid, paranoid kook who's about to be sanctioned, perhaps disbarred."

Weurster stands. "I'm outta here."

We go back to the courtroom and the judge sets the hearing for the day after tomorrow at two p.m.

CHAPTER 9

Twenty-five minutes later, I pace beneath large Impressionist murals in Andrew's waiting room. An additional 20 minutes slip by and I'm still pacing while the receptionist eyes me with increasing apprehension. Finally Andrew steps off the elevator. "Detective Moore, what are you doing here?"

I point to his office, concerned that if I say anything I'll lose it.

"Please follow me." He steps aside, allowing me to enter the office—which I do, and then slam the door as soon as he steps inside. "What are you trying to do?"

"Solve your case."

"You mean mess up my life, screw Jeanette Pore and maybe cashier your law license?"

Andrew tosses his suit jacket on the couch, loosens his tie and rolls up his sleeves as I talk. As I finish he comes over and grabs me by the hips and pulls me to him and kisses me passionately. I'm too off-guard to resist. He pulls his face away, but grasps my hips in an iron-like vise. His face is flushed, his eyes on fire. "Do you have the guts to go for it all? I don't mean just solving this stupid case. Who killed Howard Pore is irrelevant. Maybe the son-of-a-bitch slipped on the rocks, anyway. Figuring out who did it won't advance your career or make the world a better or safer place. And it sure as hell won't help Howard or Precious.

"You think I've lost it. Roostman, a mediocre mind and a mediocre man happy to play out his productive years in that cesspool in order to pick up 130 grand and a decent retirement, thinks I'm mad." Andrew's eyes become narrow slits, his voice hard. "Carol, the question in this case is not even who killed Precious Pore—not that that particular issue is unimportant. The real question is why

131

the United States Department of Justice covers for Sam Nichols. I think I know, but we'll probably never prove it.

"But why am I pushing this ball-less judge, who would no doubt roll over and give Mrs. Pore her visits if I were just a bit more reasonable and deferential? Because Mrs. Pore's visits are irrelevant. Oh, she'll get them anyway. Probably get full custody. No. I'll never prove the elements of the government's cover-up; but I'll force them to go belly-up."

I pull away. "I understand your plan, understand it very well. You set me up. You want them to believe that I know more than I do, that I fed everything to you, that I got you involved to flush them out. But you're using me to stink them out. They'll come at me with everything but the kitchen sink."

"They'll come at you with everything *including* the kitchen sink, and anything else that they think will intimidate you. But if you hang tough, sooner or later they'll deal with me—and then we'll have them."

"But for what? They'll never admit anything."

"They won't go through a Juvenile Court hearing, knowing that at any moment I can notify the media and have them down there. They don't even want to come to court to quash my subpoenas, because they'll be forced to admit that they have a file on Nichols that the judge may wish to see in chambers. If the press gets wind of any of this, there will be embarrassing questions— like who got the social workers to suggest family preservation? Who ordered Asha put on ice? And what does Asha have to say about what happened the night Precious was killed? Is the Justice Department afraid that Asha will implicate Sam Nichols in a homicide, maybe even child sexual abuse, physical abuse or maybe even plain old serious neglect, and foul up a case that they've been working on against the Illinois Attorney General for more than a year? Are you with me?"

"I'm probably as crazy as you, but yes."

He grabs me and we kiss passionately. "Let's get a hotel room and fuck our brains out," he says.

"You're crazy. I'm going back to Headquarters; or better, I'm going home and await the inevitable. If you're not disbarred and I'm not fired—well, maybe we can celebrate our good fortune."

"Yeah, good." He turns around and runs his hand through his hair and then sits back against his desk, arms folded, his mind racing far beyond fucking our brains out. "Weurster has been on the phone since she scrambled out of the courtroom, with every person on our list of witnesses. She's also talking to a few people not on the list. Pretty soon they'll be figuring who to sell out, to buy out and with how much of what. The social workers are expendable, since they probably know nothing about what went down except who told them to work out the family preservation situation. They're bigger fools, or pawns, than Lilly and Sam."

"And we're the buy-outs," I say.

"First, they'll try to scare us out, then buy us off."

"And what will they do when they discover that we can't be bought?"

"That's when the real fun begins. Heads will roll. Big heads. The folks at the top who didn't know will sacrifice everyone who did, regardless of rank, to protect their own butts."

"Anyone who sent those kids home to a thug like Sam knowing that he was dangerous should suffer the consequences of their actions," I say. "On the other hand, Sam may have killed Precious, even sexually abused her; he may have done in Howard as well. I want to get Sam."

"Without these folks protecting Sam, Lilly can be squeezed. From what you tell me, she's ripe to cash loverboy in." He pushes himself away from the desk and in two steps envelops me in his arms. "God, I want you!"

I shove him away. "Are you turned on to me or the case?"

"Don't be silly. I'm high on you and the intimacy of working so closely with you in creating something exciting. That leads to great sex."

"Your idea of intimacy and mine don't quite coincide. Let's discuss more important matters. I'll be getting a call from Captain Robertson this afternoon or tomorrow. What do you suggest I do?"

"Hang tough. We hold the high cards. Deny you know me, that you got me involved."

"And when they demote me? Will you keep me company while I work cemetery watch?"

"They won't. It won't stick once we break the case, and they know it. They'll bluster and threaten, but they won't touch you. They're sitting on the powder keg. As long as the story stays private, keeping you where you are is good damage control. Demoting you will make you a martyr, particularly once the facts come out. Hang tough and get in touch with me as soon as possible."

Andrew makes another half-hearted pass before picking up the phone and ordering an underling in. I leave, get to my car and phone Headquarters. All's quiet, so I decide to get home at a reasonable hour to spend some real time with Emily and Liam. Jeff's lying on the living room floor, tossing Liam in the air. Liam howls with glee. Emily screams, "My turn, Daddy!"

Jeffrey sees me, puts Liam down and hugs Emily. "You're too big, sweetie, for Daddy to toss you around. After I kiss Mommy, I'll give you a piggyback ride." He comes over and kisses me softly. "What gives?"

"I had enough for the day."

"Bad?"

"Bad and good."

"Want to talk about it?"

"Maybe later," I say as I pick up Liam, who had been tugging on my skirt and crying, "Mommy, pick me up." Emily is now sitting quietly on the couch with a coloring book and crayon. I sit beside her, cradling Liam on my lap. "And what are you up to, young lady?"

"A little work," she says without looking up, and continuing her charade of ignoring me.

"How's school?"

"I hate it."

Liam begins jumping around to divert my attention from Emily. "What do you guys want for dinner?" I ask.

"'Roni and cheese," Liam says.

"A grilled cheese sandwich and chips," Emily says.

"How about Shake-n-Bake?"

They both erupt into cheers of joy as if I had offered them prime rib (which, of course, they wouldn't cheer about at all).

And so I spend a sane enjoyable evening dining on Shake-n-Bake chicken, raw carrots, rice, a glass of white wine, three chocolate chip cookies and a cup of tea. I play with the kids and cuddle them, give them their baths, tuck them in to pleas of "Sleep with me, Mommy," which I do until they doze off—and all the while I ponder my other life: the bodies, sex perps, child abusers, the Lillys and Sams and Jeanette Pores, as well as the Tatles, the Byrons and the Clarence Williamses. Last of all I ruminate about my relationship with Andrew. I am almost asleep and very groggy by the time the kids doze off. I stumble into the living room.

"You look overworked, Carol. I worry about you."

"Thanks."

"I didn't mean it that way. In fact, you're more beautiful today than the day I met you."

"You're either losing your eyesight or very horny."

Jeffrey becomes serious. He's always serious, but sometimes he's *very* serious. "You have no idea. Before, you were just beautiful. Now your integrity, your character enhance your beauty."

Yeah, I think to myself, like when I'm lying on Andrew's couch. I embrace Jeffrey. "I'm sorry I've been out of sorts. This case has gotten to me."

"You try to do too much and keep it all inside. It's not healthy. You've got to slow down. Communicate more. The stress is driving you away from me—but I'm here for you, just like you've always been there for me. We're a team."

I kiss him softly. "You're a good man, Jeffrey. And I'm very tired. I'm off to bed. Someday soon, this will pass."

CHAPTER 10

I get in early, to discover that Margaret Greenspan got in even earlier. "What are you doing?" she asks when I call her back.

"Sipping coffee."

"How long will it take you to get to the teen mothers' shelter?"

"Twenty, 25 minutes."

"Patty Pearson and Jena Joslin want to see you as soon as possible."

Thirty minutes later, I'm sipping weak coffee in a small room, sitting across a cheap conference table from Joslin and Pearson. We dabble in small talk. How long have you been on the force? Where did you go to college? My Lord, from a drama major to a Homicide detective! You must be constantly depressed with what you see. And so must you; and how long have you labored in the social work vineyard? And what did you do before DCFS? Finally, I ask, "You wanted to discuss the Pore matter?"

Pearson stares at the tabletop, Joslin at the backs of her hands. Finally Joslin speaks. "I can summarize our situation, but if I misstate anything, please correct me, Patty." Pearson nods affirmatively.

"Lenore Weurster phoned yesterday afternoon. She was very agitated. Demanded to see us later this morning. Claims that we're being subpoenaed to testify in the case of Asha Pore at Juvenile Court. Wants to go over our testimony. Claims that the child's grandmother has retained a prominent attorney, Andrew Malcolm, who is arguing that we're part of a conspiracy to hide Sam and Lilly's abusive conduct and protect Sam from homicide charges. She implied that we must tailor the facts a bit here and embroider a bit there—not actually perjure ourselves, mind you; but after all the fudging and embellishing, our story will not be accurate. Ms. Weurster suggested that unless all of us are on the same page, we could be sued civilly and lose everything—possibly even be prosecuted. Not that we did anything wrong, but apparently this Malcolm fellow has a lot of power. He'll make us look evil, or at best stupid, like we did something wrong. We did not. We have always acted professionally."

"And, Ms. Moore," Pearson interjects, "we may have erred in providing the family preservation services originally, but we all make mistakes—particularly in this business, where we work with so many dysfunctional people. But we must take chances. We can't take every child from every marginal parent. The resources aren't there. Besides, many children do better with dysfunctional parents with whom they have nonetheless bonded than with foster parents, virtual strangers. And by law, we must provide services to errant parents so that they can get their lives back together. But in retrospect, we probably made a mistake in this particular case."

Joslin picks up: "In brief, we acted zealously but professionally, and will not change our testimony or our story."

Pearson looks up from the table. "Jena, let's be frank. Detective Moore, we feel that we are being set up to take the fall."

"And for what? Doing our job," Joslin sighs.

"How did you get into the case?" I ask.

"Ms. Weurster phoned. Said she had a case that cried out for Community Bound."

"Is that unusual?"

"For Weurster to call, yes. But not for someone in the State's Attorney's office to refer a case to us. We receive referrals from the State's Attorney, Public Defender, Public Guardian and our own social workers."

"Roostman did not refer this case?"

"Not as far as we know. In fact, I have the distinct impression that he knew almost nothing about it. With his caseload, he's happy if professionals step in and take care of a problem. He accepted our recommendation that Sam and Lilly receive Community Bound services."

"And that was your professional recommendation? You did not make the recommendation based solely upon Ms. Weurster's suggestion?"

"More or less," Joslin says.

"What do you mean?"

"To be frank, it was a close call. Both Sam and Lilly are heavy-duty substance abusers, not the kind turned around overnight. We expressed our concerns to Ms. Weurster, but she encouraged us to take a chance."

"Anything in writing?"

"No," Pearson replies.

"But to be fair, we've handled cases almost as difficult," Joslin says. "We have turned parents around. We've had children die on us before. Children die in foster care as well as in Community Bound, and children we send home without Community Bound die too. But after Precious died, we should have been in Juvenile Court the next day seeking custody of Asha."

"And doing a full-fledged investigation into Precious' death," Pearson says.

"So why didn't you?"

"After the child's death, we conferred with the state director of Community Bound. He told us to rely on Weurster's judgment. Weurster ordered us to take immediate custody of Asha, but not to bring the case to court. She said that she would get in touch with the parents and have a chat with them. We have the right to take protective custody for up to 48 hours before having to take the case to court. Within that 48-hour period, Weurster apparently met with Lilly, because Lilly signed a voluntary agreement giving us custody. And yes, voluntary agreements are unusual, though not unheard-of.

"Weurster wouldn't let us interview Asha until after the funeral. By that time Weurster had interviewed Asha at least twice. We don't know how long these interviews lasted, where they took place or even who was present. Asha later told us that several people were present when she talked to Weurster, at least one of whom was another woman.

"Did you ever hear of a Clarence Williams?" I ask.

"Not that I recall," Pearson says.

139

"Just a moment," Joslin says. "Didn't Sam mention a Clarence during one of our sessions?"

"That's right. We had a session with Sam and Lilly over their drinking, and Sam said something like 'Go tell it to Clarence.' Lilly told him to shut up, and that was the end of it."

I ask about their conversations with Asha without mentioning what I read in Albert and Flynn's reports.

"Without going into the content of what she told us, which is privileged and confidential…suffice it to say that she did not witness the incident."

"I understand that on occasion, she may have placed the incident in the bathroom," I say.

After a few seconds of fidgeting, Joslin responds. "That's correct. In some of her versions, she claims that she was in the living room and that Precious was burned in the bathroom. She could be confused. Ms. Moore, Detective Moore…"

"Carol."

"Carol, we performed our jobs as well as we could. We followed instructions. But the State's Attorney, not us, determines whether to screen a case into court. Right now, reading between the lines, I think we're being set up to take a fall. We'd like to explain our testimony and the background of the case to Mr. Malcolm."

I ask for a private office and phone Andrew. "They're minnows in a sea of sharks," he says.

"They're scared out of their minds. They want to cooperate with us."

"We don't need them. Besides, they've already told you everything we need to know. By the way, has Robertson been in touch with you?"

"Not that I know of."

"Hang tough."

"What about these women?"

"None of my business, at least now."

Joslin and Pearson appear stunned by the news. "I had presumed that Mr. Malcolm would be anxious to hear us out."

"He's thinking about it," I lie. "I'll be back in touch."

"Please don't leave your name, even on voicemail."

140

They're not paranoid, just realistic. Just how realistic I discover when I return to Area 5. Malone is looking through his half-open door. "Dearie, please come in and shut the door behind you."

Malone is a big, beefy, jowly man, bald on top with grey frizzy hair around his ears. He may not be the most competent detective on the force, but he's a decent man in a fatherly sort of way. He's very serious now, and apparently embarrassed by his need to be. "Something's very wrong, Carol, and it's way beyond my ability to help you." He comes out from behind his desk and sits in an ancient wooden chair next to mine, facing his desk chair. He maneuvers until he faces me. He leans over, putting his hand on my knee in a non-threatening, paternal sort of way.

"Robby phoned. He doesn't want to talk to me or to see you. Ordered you to see an Assistant United States Attorney named Joan Tatle immediately."

"That's it?"

"Not quite. He said that if you survive today, and if he does, you can forget about being a detective. He also said that that's the best that you can hope for." Malone takes his hand away and mops perspiration from his head, then plants his elbows on the armrest of the chair. He continues, "I've been on the force since before you were born. You learn to deal with the politics of the job, the jellyfish brass and the way they go belly-up to political pressure. The call I got from Robby was different. He wasn't blustering or cursing. The man was quiet. Worse, he was scared. Maybe I'm reading too much into what he said, but I think he was frightened not just for himself, but for you. Carol, there's got to be some very powerful outside forces at work. Protect yourself."

CHAPTER 11

"May I assume that you're not wearing a wire?"

"Would it make a difference?"

"Not in this room. Let me introduce myself. I'm Joan Tatle."

"And I'm Carol Moore."

"I know that."

"And I know who you are, what you are and a whole lot more."

"You're a smart cop. Maybe you should have pursued your acting career."

"Should I be intimidated because you did a background check on me? I just hope that your information includes ideas on how to get my son toilet-trained."

"Perhaps if you'd spend less time around a certain lawyer you could attend to domestic matters."

"I resent any implication that my relationship with Mr. Malcolm is anything but professional."

"At the Department of Justice, we do not hint or imply. We deal only with hard, provable reality. The facts."

"Like protecting pedophiles, child abusers and child killers?"

Tatle has been seated on a blue rayon couch facing me. I sit in a rayon-covered armchair. She flushes slightly, stands and walks behind me. I do not turn, but continue facing the couch. Tatle is about my height, with wide shoulders, long arms and a rawboned look that combine to make her appear taller. She has short dark curly hair that accentuates large ears and dark-brown eyes set wide apart in a broad face and narrow head.

"Detective Moore, you're way over your head."

"And you?"

"Don't even try to spar with me, Carol. I've been a federal prosecutor since I got out of Harvard Law School 15 years ago. I've chewed up and spat out people a lot more experienced and a lot smarter than you. I've been around long enough to know that you're scared of me, of what I represent, of the majesty of the power behind me and what all of this could do to your career, your family, even your marriage. Your bravado is theater—bad theater."

Of course she's partially correct. I am scared and I am acting, but I'm beginning to realize that so is she. "If you have such power, why bring me into this little soundproof, wireproof room to confront me all by yourself? I don't see the power and majesty of the federal government in this hole."

She comes from behind the chair and looms over me. "You think you can thumb your nose at the criminal justice system because you have a hotshot lawyer behind you? Andrew Malcolm's a good lawyer, but his power comes because he's with an established law firm. That power will corrode when we set the hounds loose. He's by himself, just like you. His wealthy partners, who depend on even wealthier corporate interests, know nothing of his involvement in this case. They'll crack down on him when the time comes, just as the CPD is about to do with you."

"Interesting," I say, and stand facing her so that only six inches separates us. "I really must be going."

"Sit down," she hisses.

"Is that an order?"

"Not from me. The CPD sent you here."

"Okay, I'm here."

She backs off and sits on the couch. I ease back into the chair. "Detective Moore, you're close to obstructing justice."

"By investigating a murder?"

"Whose murder?"

"From your point of view, what difference does it make? A murder's a murder."

"The Justice Department is involved in a major investigation. Your actions are on the verge of compromising two years of blood, sweat, tears and a lot of money."

144

"Perhaps you should be talking to Andrew Malcolm."

"In time, perhaps; but Malcolm won't do anything without you."

"You overestimate my influence on Mr. Malcolm."

"I'll table the more personal side of that equation, at least for now. But professionally, Malcolm can't proceed without a client, and Jeanette Pore will do whatever you tell her."

"Assuming that to be true, why should I?"

"To protect a very high-level, very important federal law enforcement investigation."

"And what does Ms. Pore get?"

"Ultimately, custody of her grandchild. For now, supervised visits."

"And Sam Nichols gets away with murder."

"Sam Nichols, along with his girlfriend, neglected and more than likely abused her children. If he had a hand in this child's death, the CPD will no doubt uncover that fact with Lilly Higgins' assistance, when she's ready."

"She'll crack sooner if Asha is placed in a pediatric ecology center where she can tell the experts what really went down."

"Asha wasn't in the kitchen when the tragic accident occurred."

"You know a great deal about a state criminal case, for a federal prosecutor."

"It's all part of the federal investigation."

"Like using Sam to get information on the Attorney General, which could lead to a very high-profile indictment and garner a lot more publicity than the prosecution of a nobody for killing a nobody kid?"

"You should've skipped the force and gone straight to the pulpit."

"We're going in circles, Ms. Tatle."

"Are you prepared for the heat?"

"That's my business and my problem."

"And your family, assuming it stays together when everything comes out? Speak to your good friend, Mr. Malcolm. Apprise him of our conversation. Here's my card. He can call if he figures out a compromise that we can live with."

I call Andrew from my car phone and get a "We can't talk on the phone. I don't even trust my office. Meet me outside the Greek restaurant at Halsted and Adams in an hour."

At the appointed hour, I ease my unmarked but easily identifiable police vehicle into a No-Parking zone a half-block from the restaurant. Andrew paces back and forth in front. "Hi," he says and kisses me on the cheek, giving me a hug as he does so.

"Andrew, what are you doing?"

"Friends kiss." He studies the street, the traffic and the pedestrians and then flags a cab. "Get in," he says as it pulls up. We do, and he tells the cabby to take us to a downtown hotel.

"Have you lost your mind?"

"Not yet." He swivels to look out the rear window.

"Where are we going?"

"The hotel."

"I heard that. Why?"

"To meet someone."

"Who?"

"Jack Ryan."

"Ryan?"

"Chief Investigator for the Attorney General."

"Captain Jack Ryan? Why?"

"He's a mover and shaker. Gets things done."

"He's a greaser and oiler."

"That's what I said. He gets things done. But he's not dishonest. If Byron and Bob the Hammer are up to no good, you can bet your mortgage that Ryan knows nothing about it."

From what I've heard about Ryan, that would be accurate— but only because he chooses not to know. I get to more urgent matters. "Tatle wants to talk to you directly."

"I've nothing for her, nor she us. We—your investigation, my case—are one point in the spectrum. A second is a federal investigation of Byron and Hamilton that has retarded a child abuse investigation and may have ultimately led to the death of a child and that child's father. If so, Weurster, Tatle, Johnson and their bosses have committed far more heinous crimes than the people they were investigating. Taking kickbacks pales in comparison to placing an innocent child at risk and then covering up her murder. Ironically, one man, the possible child killer and molester, is in a position to send the whole damn lot of them away."

We pull up in front of the hotel and Andrew shoves a bill at the cabby: "Keep the change." He grabs my hand and pulls me out of the cab. We hustle through the revolving door and race to an elevator. We get off at the top floor and walk up and down the corridor to make sure that no one is around before going to the room where Ryan awaits us.

Jack Ryan, a tall slender man with neatly combed white hair and a bushy white mustache, is expensively if somewhat too formally dressed for a cop: a blue Brooks Brothers-type suit, white shirt, cufflinks, navy tie highlighted by soft cream-colored jagged lines, and cordovan wingtips. He stands as we enter. "A drink?" he asks after the introductions.

"Diet Coke, " Andrew says.

I take carbonated water, and Ryan pulls one of those little one-drink bourbon bottles from the small refrigerator. He pours the contents into a glass of ice, swirls it around several times while holding it up to the afternoon sun seeping into the room. "So the Feds are up Byron's ass?"

"So we surmise," Andrew says. We sit on a couch opposite Ryan, a glass-top coffee table separating us.

"Let's hear it from the top," Ryan says.

Andrew repeats the story almost verbatim as I had given it to him several days ago. Then he turns to me. "Detective Moore can fill us in on what occurred today."

As I talk, Ryan picks up the still-untasted bourbon and rolls the glass around in his large bony hands. When I finish, he looks at Andrew with a grin on his lips and a smile in his eyes. "The Feds, State's attorney and DCFS, and hence the governor, have got their collective tits in a great big wringer, and you're in a position to squeeze just as hard as you want."

"Or let go," Andrew says.

"For an appropriate *quid pro quo*," Ryan replies.

"So what's your take on this?" Andrew asks.

"Kickbacks. I've heard rumors. You get goons like that guy Nichols to act as informants. If they don't cooperate, they do big time. Then you pay Nichols a lot of money for bullshit information and force him to kick most of it back. The informant can't do anything about it. If he doesn't cooperate, he ends up in the joint. By cooperating, he ends up with some cash in his pocket. Besides, if he went to anyone, who'd believe him?

"But your Mr. Nichols is so dumb that he kept dealing drugs, and the Feds collared him on a different beef. Then he began blabbing to avoid doing big federal time. So they make him their informant. They wired him. They may have enough now to get the Hammer—but shit, they had enough to get him a few years ago. He's small potatoes. They want to bury him under a mountain of evidence. When they do, they'll squeeze him to get Byron. Byron's the guy they want. If they indict Hammer, they get a second-page story for a day. If they get Byron, they'll have headlines for months."

"Would Hamilton help them?" Andrew asks.

"Is there honor among thieves? In any event, it hasn't happened yet, or they wouldn't be protecting Nichols. Obviously a lot of informants are getting money and kicking back, but they don't know each other. So the Feds are figuring out who these other informants are. They may even have one or two of them, but not enough. If Mr. Nichols' personal problems become public, any case against the Hammer goes down the toilet. You can imagine the field day that a good lawyer like yourself would have, cross-examining Mr. Nichols with the truth.

"But it wouldn't go that far. The Hammer would never go on trial; and besides, a Special Prosecutor would be appointed to investigate how Department of Justice personnel became involved in this little cover-up—not to mention State's Attorney's lawyers and high-ranking DCFS officials. Byron and Hamilton would be forgotten."

Ryan finally puts his glass to his lips and consumes the entire amount. "It's delicious. Absolutely delicious. And Tatle didn't initiate this cover-up by herself. No doubt she conferred with and got the okay from Washington. And that Assistant State's Attorney was probably not the original go-to person. Tatle, or her Washington supervisors, probably went right to the State's Attorney, who passed it on to Weurster. Also, rather than Weurster going to these two Community Bound workers first, she probably went through the governor's office to assure that Community Bound got the case.

"When that baby died, or more likely was murdered, everyone involved from Justice to the State's Attorney to Community Bound had good reason to make it all go away. But Detective Moore, and now you, Andrew, have checkmated them. They have no way out, other than to kill you both—which they might consider in their darker moments. But in their more intelligent moments, they'd quickly realize that murdering you would only create more problems for them."

"You're not serious?" I ask.

"Ms. Moore, you're talking about the careers of some pretty powerful, well-connected, utterly self-absorbed individuals. If all this comes out, they'll fall from the highest pinnacles of power to the depths of its sewers. So to their minds, the necessary end justifies any means." He hesitates. "But you asked to see me. How can I help?"

"I think you already know," Andrew says.

"I do. I assume you want me to act as your agent in this matter?"

"You got it," Andrew says.

"The unpleasant specter of Mr. Nichols keeps creeping into the picture. But you're the police officer, Detective Moore. How do you feel about a potential compromise?"

I've been trying to figure out where Andrew is coming from and where Ryan is going. They speak a language the words of which I know, but the meaning eludes me. And though I do not understand the language, I infer nasty undertones. "I'm investigating one murder, and there's ample evidence that an even more heinous one may have been committed. Worse, government officials seem to be covering up both murders."

"A fair conclusion. But it can also be argued that this little family deserved to be preserved. This was a social work decision upon which the lawyers relied—which also explains why these two ladies have good reason to fear being tossed to the wolves.

"Then the lawyers and pols will argue that they removed the older daughter as soon as the child was killed. They'll point out that they had every intention of bringing the appropriate charges against Mr. Nichols at the appropriate time: the very instant that the State's Attorney obtained sufficient evidence to convict him of the heinous act of child murder."

"That's absurd," I say.

"Of course," Andrew says, "but Jack has a point. I'd like him to explore solutions."

"He has less than 24 hours."

"The less time the better," Ryan says. "That gives our opponents little wiggle room. They agree to our terms or risk consequences worse to them than death: disgrace and exclusion from the comfortable little professional communities and social circles."

"I'm still investigating a homicide," I say.

"As you should; and hopefully you'll get your killer, Ms. Moore," Ryan says as he stands. "Now, if you'll excuse me, I have work to do. Can I reach you at the numbers you previously gave me?" he asks Andrew.

"Yes."

"We'll talk in several hours. Just shut the door behind you," he says and leaves.

We stand side by side facing the door that Ryan just closed. I turn to Andrew to find myself in his arms. I push him away. "It's neither the time nor the place, and I'm not the woman."

"What's that supposed to mean?"

"Figure it out."

"You seemed happy in my arms a couple of days ago."

"Then I thought you had character."

Andrew throws his hands in the air, turns his back and comes around again to face me. "You've got to be kidding!"

"Actually, I'm not."

"So we go ahead with the hearing. The best possible outcome is the judge lets all the evidence in, the witnesses testify honestly, Jeanette gets her visits, Asha implicates Sam, Sam gets indicted and Tatle, Weurster and their friends get fired. Worst case: Roostman lets nothing in, we appeal and a year from now the Appellate Court agrees with Roostman. In the meantime, the media pays no attention to what they consider two conspiracy nuts."

"And what do you expect Mr. Ryan will accomplish?"

"Get us Sam and get Jeanette Asha."

"And the others?"

150

"There's just the two of us, Carol."

"I must go," I say.

"Stay a while."

"If I do, I'll stay too long."

"Then stay too long."

"Not today." And probably never.

CHAPTER 12

At nine o'clock I'm lying down with Liam, trying to soothe him into the world of Wynken, Blynken and Nod, though as usual I am making the transition while Liam chatters away wanting more "Three Little Piggies and Goldilocks." The phone rings and a few seconds later, Jeff informs me that "Some fellow named Andrew wants to talk to you."

"Mr. Malcolm?" I say, acting confused for the benefit of Jeffrey, still hanging around within earshot.

Andrew gets right to the point. "I've had several conversations with Jack Ryan. Things are progressing, but with a glitch here and there that ought to be resolved. In case we need you, will you be around tonight?"

"As near as my phone or pager."

"Great."

"And, Mr. Malcolm..."

"Yes?"

"Will this matter get resolved?"

"No doubt about it."

"I'll be here."

"What's that all about?" Jeffrey asks when I hang up.

"The case. What else?"

"Who's Andrew Malcolm?"

"A lawyer. He represents the mother of the man whose murder I'm investigating. And I don't want to discuss the case. I'm worn-out, physically, mentally, and I need some sleep."

But not for long. At 1:10 a.m. the pager jars me from a deep slumber. I don't recognize the number, but call back.

"Detective Moore?"

153

"Yes."

"Lilly Higgins here."

"At one in the morning?"

"I'm in deep shit."

"How can I help?"

"You're trying to finger Howard's killer. I can give you the person who did Howard in, and also killed my daughter. And I can also prove that those asshole federal cops protected Sam."

"Why the conversion?"

"You know damn well. The Feds figure they're gonna get screwed 'cause they protected me and Sam. Now they're gonna sell us out to protect their asses."

"I thought you didn't like me."

"I don't. So what?"

"Tomorrow morning?"

"We're to meet with some broad named Tatle and the State's Attorney at seven o'clock. I've gotta see you now."

"Where?"

"Here."

"Where's here?"

"My place."

"What about Sam?"

"Out whorin'."

"He may come home."

"Not a chance."

"I'm willing to see you, but not where Sam could show up."

"How long it take you to get here?"

"Half-hour tops."

"I'll be in the entrance to the building in 30 minutes. Pull up and flash your lights. We'll go someplace and talk."

"See you."

"What's that all about?" Jeff asks sleepily.

"I have to go."

He's wide-awake. "Christ, Carol."

"Sorry."

"Are you sure it's job-related?"

"What do you mean?"

"That wasn't Andrew or Tommy?"

"Will you quit being such a jealous fool and let me do my job?"

"I'm sorry. But why must you go out in the middle of the night?"

"Men, male detectives, have done it for years."

"You have two babies and a husband."

"And a lot of detectives who go out in the middle of the night have babies and wives and never come back. I'm meeting a very important female witness and I'll be in a very safe place. I fully intend to come back."

"I'll go with you."

"And Liam and Emily?"

"Shouldn't you at least have a backup?"

"Of course, but there's no one—at least no one I trust."

"What about that Welch fellow?"

"Good idea," I say, pulling on my jeans. I slip on a pair of Nikes and my shoulder holster with my .9mm. I shove a small .22 into the back of my belt. I grab a pair of handcuffs and shove them inside my jacket.

"You're pretty well-armed for a so-called no-brainer."

"I'm careful. Hopefully I'll be home in a couple of hours."

"Carol?"

"Yes?"

"I love you."

"And I love you too, Jeffrey." I lean over and kiss him on the cheek.

He grabs me and pulls me on top of him. "No, Carol, I really love you."

Now he decides to kiss me passionately, and I push myself away from him. "Jeffrey, I really love you too. Please, just let me go."

I find Welch's home phone number and call him as soon as I'm in the car, but all I get is an answering machine. "Tommy, this is Carol Moore. It's about 1:30 and I'm on my way to meet Lilly Higgins. I'm picking her up and we're going someplace away from Sam, probably a Thai restaurant that's open until four at Lawrence and Broadway. She claims that she's gonna give me Sam. It should be okay, but I'd feel safer with some kind of backup. I'm picking her up at 432 West Winthrop and should be at the Thai restaurant in about a half an hour. If you get this message, please meet me there. Otherwise I'll call back in an hour or so."

I unholster my .9mm as I pull up to Lilly's building and cradle it in my jacket pocket. I flash the lights. Lilly bounds out of her foyer, quickly opens the passenger-side door and slides in next to me. "Let's go." I let go of the gun and grab the steering wheel with both hands—stupidly.

"Just ease up and keep your hands on the wheel." I do what she says, since the gun that she holds is pressed to my temple. She pulls my weapon from the jacket, "Boy, you're one dumb motherfucking cop. Now, real slow, move your left hand off the wheel and unlock the doors."

I do, and my door quickly opens. Sam grabs me by the back of my neck and pulls me from the car. "March."

"Where?"

He throws a hammerlock around me. "Into our place. Maybe you'll get lucky and get it on with a real man." He shoves me.

"Wait a second," Lilly says.

"Huh?"

"What if she's got another weapon?"

"You got it already."

"I got one, stupid. Maybe she's got another one."

"Yeah, you're right. Put your hands on your head, broad."

Lilly shakes her head. "Move it, bitch."

Once inside the apartment, they lead me to the living room. A dim light barely illuminates the room. "Can I put my hands down?"

"Not yet." Lilly moves behind me, shoving the gun into the back of my head. I try to sort out what's happening and what my chances are of ever changing Liam's diapers again, of snuggling with Emily, of trying to salvage my relationship with Jeffrey or of finally ending my not-yet-affair with Andrew.

"Search her," Lilly barks. He rips the front of my shirt off and begins to paw at my breasts.

"You fucking animal! Cut it out. Or as God is my witness, I'll kill you," Lilly screams.

"Just having a little fun, Lil. See, she's got another weapon here. A little one."

"Not as little as your dick," I blurt out without thinking.

"Wanna see the biggest fuckin' piece of meat this side of a horse?"

"No, she doesn't. Just finish the job," Lilly barks.

He does, grabbing my crotch for good measure. "Just a pair of cuffs."

"Get your hands down and put them behind you," Lilly says. I do and she snaps the cuffs on.

"I don't like this," Sam says.

"What's there not to like?"

"That broad in our flat."

"Not for long."

"Why can't we just take her down to the lake and get rid of her?"

"It ain't that easy," Lilly says.

"You call me dumb, but them assholes tell us to take the copper here are stupid sons-of-bitches, and you for listening to them."

"Those assholes are our meal ticket."

"I'm your meal ticket, baby."

"Shut up."

"Says who?"

"Says me, and I've got a big gun in my hand."

"You gonna kill me, the broad and get rid of both bodies? You're one fuckin' genius."

Lilly lies back on the couch. "Sit down, bitch. We could be in for a long evening."

I ease myself into a chair. Sam disappears to come back in a few minutes with a bottle of cheap bourbon. He flops in a large low chair and takes a long swig from the bottle. "I say we have some fun with the bitch."

Lilly stares at the ceiling like she's in a world by herself. Sam stands, throws his head back and gulps down another six ounces or so. He swaggers over till he stands over me menacingly, a filthy, stinking, rotten example of the lowest rung of the human species. Christ, what a way to die! I cling to the precarious hope that Welch got my message and is not wasting time at the Thai restaurant.

Sam grabs my armpits and pulls me up. He unbuckles my belt and begins to pull my jeans down. I thrust my knee into his crotch with all my strength. It's not enough. He's totally unfazed and takes a step back. "You like the rough stuff, huh, baby?"

I spit in his face. If I'm to die, I'm going out as tough as I can.

Sam wipes the saliva from his face. He pulls his beefy and powerful arms back, but before he can smash his fists into my face, Lilly shouts, "Sam, you touch her and I'll blow your worthless balls off."

He turns to Lilly, who's sitting up with the gun trained on him. "Since when did you get so highfalutin' moral?"

"Since your friends told us their plan."

"Yeah, but you did the talking. I'm too dumb, remember?"

"You're not stupid, Sam, just impulsive."

"If you think I'm gonna stand here and let this whore cop knee me and spit in my face, you're as dumb a fuckin' bitch as she is."

"You assaulted her, tried to assault her."

"And she deserved it. The bitch wouldn't listen to reason. Tried to put us away. Maybe even get you the death chamber."

"She was just doing her fuckin' job. Besides, they don't want no bruises and no sexual assaults."

"I didn't hear that."

"Because I talked to them."

"I don't trust their fancy asses."

"Me neither, Sam. But they got just as much reason as us to be rid of her, and they know a lot better than us how to get away with it."

"Fuck you, Lilly, and fuck them. I didn't do nothin' wrong."

"What about the sale of illegal drugs, Sam? And the little matter of diddling with little kids?"

"And what about killing Precious and her Dad?" I ask.

He pivots back to me sticking his face into mine. "You know fucking nothing! I never killed nobody in my whole fuckin' life. At least not until now, bitch."

"So Precious took a pot of water from the stove and carried it into the bathroom, where she poured it on top of herself. It won't fly. It will all come out, even if you kill me. They'll get you, Sam."

Sam's face grows purple. The veins in his nose are about to pop. I know I'm dead for sure. Will it hurt? Will I suffer the indignity of a rape? What will happen to Liam and Emily? Will Jeff, after an appropriate period of mourning, take my police pension and marry some bimbo graduate student? Will Andrew get his compromise, or will my death blow everything? And will he find some other dissatisfied woman to bed down? And I'll bet I'm not the first—something I have never considered before. How will Lilly and Sam fare as long as Andrew is on the case? But as long as Lilly and Sam are alive, Tatle, Weurster and her friends are in deep shit — unless, of course, Andrew is part of what is going down? But that is impossible. But how can anything be worked out as long as Lilly and Sam are alive? And then it hits me.

As Sam continues to stare at me, it's clear that he is trying to figure the situation out. He turns and in two steps he's on the couch. He slaps Lilly hard across the face and grabs the gun from her. "Where's the copper's guns?"

"Sam."

"Give 'em to me."

"Under the cushions."

He shoves her off the couch, lifts up the cushion and grabs my two guns. "Now I've got all the guns and all the bullets and I'm gonna have me some fun and then blow this copper away and let the assholes worry about it, 'cause they're the smart ones." He tosses the guns onto the chair where I had been sitting.

"You're both fools," I say, talking rapidly.

"You sound scared, copper—and you should be."

"So should you."

"Whaddaya mean?"

"You're being set up."

"Fuck you," Sam says, but he's listening.

"These fools need you out of the way a lot more than they need me gone. I got very little, but you know everything. You know that the Hammer and the Attorney General have been taking kickbacks. That could put them in jail. You know that Weurster and the FBI guys have protected you from child abuse and murder charges. That could give them an even longer jail term. If they let you live, you're in a position to blackmail them for the rest of their lives."

"Fuckin' right."

"Yeah, but do you think they'll stop at killing a cop? What do you think you mean to them? Do you think anyone would be interested if they find all of our bodies here?"

Sam looks at Lilly. "The bitch's got something."

"Don't listen to her, Sam. She's scared out of her mind. She'll say anything."

"But why'd they want us to bring the broad here?"

"That's right, Sam," I say. "You kill me, it eliminates one minor irritant. Then they come on the scene and kill you trying to get away after killing me."

"Irritant? What's that?"

Christ, I'm about to die and I'm giving this moron a vocabulary lesson. "A minor problem. After you do away with me, they come in and blow you two away. Bingo! End of problem. Detective Moore killed by a thug, the man who killed Howard Pore and his girlfriend, and they, whoever they are, kill you. They're heroes, and everyone who can say anything about their dealing is dead."

"The bitch is right," Sam says.

"The bitch is...What difference does it make? We've gotta kill her. The faster, the better. Then you and me will beat it before anyone gets here."

"Beat it? To where? With what?" Sam asks.

"Sam, kill the bitch and let's get outta here!"

"Yeah. But first I'm gonna have me some fun. I'm gonna butt-fuck the bitch."

"Sam."

"Who cares about sperm or marks?" He spins me around and pulls my jeans down to my knees. "Great fucking buns. I'm gonna enjoy this!"

"You fucking animal," Lilly screams.

"Fuck you, cunt," Sam says without looking at her. He's too busy pulling his pants down.

Lilly struggles off the floor and stumbles to the chair. She grabs her gun. "No more, Sam. I've had it with you."

"Fuck..." which is the last word that Sam Nichols mutters in his relatively brief but entirely worthless life. Lilly sends a round into his jaw, causing blood, bone and part of his tongue to cascade over my neck and shoulders. I fall on my knees and roll over in time to see Sam lunge ineffectively at Lilly. He hits the floor, moaning. Using his massive strength, he pulls himself up on all fours and crawls after her, but Lilly stands her ground. He gets to her feet. She puts the gun to his head. "The first shot was for me. This one's for Precious." Boom! The second shot sends Sam's soul to its ultimate fate.

CHAPTER 13

Lilly stands, walks around the room as if she's expecting someone. She goes back to where Sam's body lies and slumps to the floor next to it. She slowly picks the gun up and cradles it to her body. She looks at me. "I didn't do that for you, Carol. It was for me, and it was what I was supposed to do after he killed you. Yeah, that's the plan. And it made no difference if he beat you or raped you first. I just had enough of that shit. I couldn't sit here and watch him fuck no one no more. But now I goofed, since I've killed him before he could kill you. Now when I kill you I'll have the gun residue on my hand. It was supposed to be on his.

"But it makes no difference, 'cause you're right. They made me promises. But shit, they can't have me hanging around, 'cause who knows what I might say after too much booze." Lilly laughs hollowly and without mirth. "Look at us. We're two beauties. Your boobs hanging out and your pants down with Sam's blood all over you. And me sitting in his stinking mess. I hate you, Carol, 'cause you're everything I should be. I got brains and my tits and ass are, or were, every bit as good as yours. Shit, we could be sisters. But when you were getting educated with books and decent guys and getting on the police force, I was getting educated by selling my body and fucking assholes. It's a rotten world, Carol, but you might survive this shit if they let you.

Not me. I'm dead."

"Not yet," I say, trying to figure out words to slow her down. But my voice rings hollow, unconvincing.

"Soon. Real soon. And I should pay for my crime. Yeah, the asshole was right. He didn't kill nobody ever—at least as far as I know. *I* killed my baby daughter." Lilly looks down at Sam's corpse and shakes her head sadly. "No one knew but Sam and me. Those social workers didn't want to know, and neither did the cops; but they suspected Sam. And if it weren't for Sam, Precious would be alive. I caught Sam fingering her twice. I told him to cut it out. Said I'd kill him if I caught him again. And then I caught him in the bathroom with her. I went crazy. I wanted to kill Sam, but couldn't. Didn't know how. So I went into the kitchen and grabbed the water, which was just boiling. I went into the bathroom. 'You want her? Take her. Take her like this,' and just poured the boiling water all over my poor little darling.

"Then we panicked. We rubbed Vaseline on her for hours. Finally, when she was dying we took her to the hospital, too late. That's it, Carol. I killed my own flesh." She laughs hollowly. "I don't want to live. Will I go to Hell, or will God feel sorry for me 'cause I ain't all that evil, even if I killed Precious and Sam?"

Lilly puts the gun in her mouth.

"Lilly, listen to me," I say. "Sam deserved to die. You saved my life. And you were insane when you killed Precious. Sam drove you to it."

She pulls the gun from her mouth. "You think so?"

"Yes, yes."

"So do I—but it don't make no difference. Those folks will kill me anyway."

"Not if we get out of here. Besides, we've got the firepower."

"Carol, I'm beginning to like you. I could be you if I didn't have a drunk for a Mom, a jerk for a Dad and a sex pervert for a stepdad. But you're naïve. Those folks call the shots in this world. They chew up people like me—and you too, whether you know it or want to admit it or not."

"Who are these folks? Who called you tonight?

Lilly smiles sadly. She stands and disappears for a half-minute. She returns with a roll of duct tape. She cuts a long piece and wraps it tightly around my mouth. She flops down next to Sam's body.

"I'm going where clout don't count." She sticks the gun in her mouth. I see her thumb tightening on the trigger and jam my eyes shut as the blast blows the back of her head off.

I don't know whether to cry out of happiness that at least for the moment I'm still alive, or out of a terrible sadness from what I've just heard and seen. But I don't cry. I just scrunch myself back up so that I'm resting against the chair. I try to ease myself into a position where my arms do not ache, at least not as much as they do now. I have a very faint glimmer of hope that Tommy will show up and an even slimmer one that the neighbors have heard the shots and called the cops. But in this neighborhood, gunshots in the middle of the night are seldom reported. I think of pounding my feet on the floor, but that'll probably get only hollering from the people below. Nevertheless, I'm about to try when I hear the doorknob turn and the door open.

A man of medium height and build enters. His dark hair is slicked-back and greying at the edges. He wears a cream-colored sport jacket, a brown sportshirt open at the neck, tan slacks and loafers. He glances at me and then quickly looks away. I recognize but can't place him. I kick my feet on the floor, but he doesn't seem to notice.

He walks over to the bodies, shaking his head. He bends over and takes the gun still dangling from Lilly's hand and maneuvers it so that her index finger is on the trigger. Still holding her hand, with the gun now in it, he turns to me. This time the gun is pointed at my head. I clamp my eyes shut and await the inevitable for the second time in less than half an hour. This time I'm almost resigned.

"Bob the Hammer Hamilton."

Tommy Welch leans against the doorway. Hamilton looks at Welch, back at me and then at Tommy again.

"What are you doing with that gun?" Welch asks.

Hamilton drops Lilly's hand and stands; this time he's holding the weapon. Welch ignores him, takes off his UAW jacket exposing his still-holstered .38 police special and walks over to me. He puts the jacket around my naked upper body and gently lifts me up. He then pulls up my jeans. All the time I'm making noises through the tape. Why the devil can't he just take the tape off? "Geez, sorry, kid; I wasn't thinking," Tommy says, and finally takes the tape off.

"Tommy, that man will kill you."

165

"Bob the Hammer may be kinky, but he's not stupid—are you, Bob?" Welch says without turning around.

"I dunno what the broad's talking about."

"He was about to kill me."

"You're fucking crazy."

"Why did you leave me like this and then point the gun at me?"

"Why should I help you? What are you, a fucking whore friend of Lilly's or one of Sam's lays? I was gonna keep you just like that till I got the CPD."

"Get me out of these cuffs."

Tommy pulls a pick from his pocket, and in three seconds my hands are loose. I lunge at Hamilton, stupidly, because he's still holding the gun. Welch grabs me before I get to him. "Leave it go, Carol."

"He's a fucking crook. He's a fucking murderer!" I scream.

Welch stands between me and Hamilton. "Put the gun down, Bob." Hamilton does.

"Why you here?" Welch asks him.

"This here guy lying on the floor, Sam Nichols, is an informant for our BADD unit. I found out tonight that he's also working for the US Attorney's office trying to prove that Byron and me are taking kickbacks. I came up here to talk to him about that and walked into this little mess. Who the fuck is she?"

"Detective Carol Moore," Welch says. "She's been working on a murder case in which your previously reliable informant was no doubt involved. Sit down, Hammer."

"Says who?"

"Hammer, you're in enough shit already. Just sit down and shut up." Hamilton sits in the couch above the two bodies. Welch walks over to the phone and pushes in a number. "Ollie. Yeah, I know it's fucking three in the morning. I'm here with Detective Moore. Remember her? Yeah, I know what she looks like. But she doesn't look too good right now. Bob the Hammer's here too. Don't ask me. I don't know. But I'm also staring at two bodies whose heads are blown apart. Yeah, I haven't called 911 yet. Call Robby and tell him to get his butt down here. I'll give you 15 minutes, and then I'm gonna dial 911."

The rest is a blur. Robertson pulls Hammer and myself into a bedroom, where he, Ollie Tate and two other official-looking types begin to grill me. Welch rambles in. "Get out of here, Welch," Robertson says. Tommy ignores him and goes to a corner of the room, where he leans against a wall. "You understand the English language?"

"Certainly, Captain, but this is my case, too, and I'm entitled to be here."

Robertson, who has been sitting on the bed next to me, turns and glares at him. "This is not your case, and I for one would like to know why you're here."

"For starters, I'm sure that the CPD will want my report on how Bob the Hammer was about to blow away one of Chicago's finest."

Hamilton, who has been sitting in a corner, leaps up and takes a couple of steps at Tommy. "No one talks about me that way."

"Why'd you stop? No one's holding you back," Welch says, without taking himself from the wall.

"I wouldn't waste my muscle on the likes of a down-and-out crumb cop like you."

"You're absolutely right, Hammer; save your strength for Stateville. You'll need it to protect your white asshole."

This time Hamilton lunges at Welch, who again doesn't move. Tate and another of the official-looking fellows grab Hamilton and sit him back down.

"Okay, okay; everyone calm down," Robby says and ignores Welch. "Let's hear your story from the top." So I give Robertson the version of facts starting with Lilly's phone call to me. I do not mention the meeting with Ryan, or Andrew's involvement.

When I finish, Robby taps his pencil on his notebook. "Someone higher than me will have to sort out this mess. In the meantime, Moore, you did okay. Take a couple of days off and get your nerves in working order. When you come back, report to Traffic."

"Traffic?" I ask.

"We don't want you in Homicide. It was stupid to walk into a situation like this by yourself, without a backup."

"But..."

"You heard me." He stands and starts out the door. I move in front of him and block his way. "Detective Moore, let me by."

"Listen, you son-of-a-bitch, I'm not about to take any shit from you or anyone else after what I've been through tonight."

"Detective Moore, you have been through a lot, and I am taking all of that into account. I won't have you up on discipline. But you will report to Traffic. End of discussion."

We stand facing each other. I'm so pissed off that I'm ready to strangle him. Ollie Tate moves over and places his hand on my shoulder. "Carol, go home. After a few days the captain will think differently."

Robertson turns around to him. "Ollie..."

In the meantime Welch walks over, sits on the bed, picks up the phone and dials. "What are you doing?" Robertson asks.

"I'm calling..." and he mentions the name of a prominent columnist with the *Tribune*.

"Put that phone down."

"The guy told me to call him at home any time I got a juicy story."

Robertson flies at Welch, grabs the phone out of his hand and slams it onto the receiver. Tommy looks at him but talks to me. "Carol, leave the room and take everyone with you except Ollie. Ollie, Captain Robertson and I want to have a little chat."

We get out quickly. Ten minutes later I'm called back in. "I apologize, Detective Moore," Robertson says. "I was out of line. But neither you, nor your friends here, Sergeant Tate and Detective Welch, can know the pressure I'm under, that we commanders can be under. Take your time off and report back to Homicide."

"With a recommendation for a department award," Welch says.

"Yeah, that's right," Robertson says, stands and comes over. "You did a good job, Carol. I don't know if I'm supposed to hug a female detective or just shake her hand."

"Given my present condition, a handshake will do," I say. He shakes my hand and is out the door.

"Would you mind leaving the room?" I ask Welch. "I'd better give my husband a call."

"Carol, where you been? I've been worried sick," Jeff says.

"There's been a little glitch."

"Anything serious?"

"Two dead bodies."

"Are you okay?" he gasps.

"Physically, yes—except for blood and tissue splattered around my body and hair. I'll be home soon."

"I'll wake the kids up and we'll pick you up."

"Tommy will drive me home."

"Welch?"

"Yes. See you soon."

"Give me your keys," Tommy says when I come out of the room. He gets a description of the car and gives the keys to a cop to drive it home. The photographers are still taking pictures, and the evidence techs are dusting the room down, though there's really no reason to do so.

"Want to talk about it?" Welch asks as we pull away.

"No."

"I mean the whole thing."

"Not now. But thanks for saving my life."

"Don't know if I did, except with Robby."

"That Hammer fellow would have killed me."

"We'll never know."

I look past the windshield, where the wipers slowly and methodically swish away a soft rain. Uptown's streets and buildings look bleaker than usual. Tommy's right. I'll never know what went down. For certain, Ryan had a very busy evening. No doubt he spoke to Tatle and either Weurster or her bosses, and probably someone in the governor's office about DCFS involvement. Could even have gone to Byron and Hamilton and laid it all out. Someone had the idea of getting rid of Lilly and Sam by setting me up. Sam would kill me. Lilly would nail Sam, and Hamilton would dispose of Lilly. Case closed. And Hamilton could have been acting for himself and Byron — or, for that matter, for Tatle and Weurster, or even Ryan, or all of them. Except Andrew, of course. But Lilly, poor Lilly shafted them. She may not have been a prize, but at the end she died with dignity.

And now Sam won't stand trial on child abuse charges; or, assuming that he did kill Howard, on that case either. Nor will Lilly. There may not even be a bribery case against Byron and Hamilton. I wonder what Andrew will do now, what he'll think of Ryan's machinations.

But then I recall Andrew's call to me earlier in the evening. Would I be reachable by phone or pager? Lilly couldn't phone me, of course, since she had no way of knowing my unlisted phone number; but I did give her my card with my pager on it. My heart begins to thump loudly. Could Andrew have set me up? I shove the thought aside. But he could have been the unwitting tool in a game that he didn't understand—or want to understand. But no; certainly Andrew who lay with me on the couch would never sell me out. For what? No, it's impossible. I cannot believe that he would do that or allow it to be done. Suddenly I'm so very, very tired.

We pull up in the driveway. Welch comes around and opens the door for me. "That's very un-Tommy Welch," I say.

Tommy looks at me with a very un-Tommy Welch look, which embarrasses me. When he realizes that I'm embarrassed, he becomes awkward. "I'm around if you need me, kid."

"I know that, Tommy—and thanks."

"For nothin'," he laughs.

"No, Tommy; thanks for being Tommy."

Jeffrey comes out of the front door and throws his arms around me. "I just heard it on the news. God, you're a mess!"

I take Jeffrey's arm. Tommy gets in the car, flashes his lights and drives away.

CHAPTER 14

A week later, I'm back on the job. I check my calls and one is from someone named Brenda, a patient at Cook County Hospital. I call back and find out that she's on an AIDS ward and close to death. Although I don't recall the name, I figure that I'd better see her, which I do later in the day. Brenda lies in a bed surrounded by bags of gook, out of which pour medicine and sustenance into her arms and legs.

"Be good seeing you, dearie. Remember me? I be Brenda, Howard Pore's girlfriend. I'm about used up, ready to cash it in, so I figure I better come clean. Don't want to go on to the next world—theres is a next world, isn't there, dearie?—without lettin' you know what happened to poor Howard.

"Howard and me, we be fuckin' on the rocks and drinkin' wine and shootin' up some bad shit. When we be gettin' ready to go, Howard fall backwards, hit his head and rolls into the lake. The lake was real wild. I tried to get to him but he was gone, lost in the dark.

"I didn't be killin' him. Actually, I loved Howard—as much as I've ever loved anyone, that is. But I'm just a poor nigger who'll get stuck at 26th and California on some beef that I didn't do. But now, that's it, dearie. You ain't gonna do nothin' about it, are you?"

I slowly drive back to headquarters, thinking about the case and about Andrew, who hasn't phoned me since he called and asked about my pager. Maybe he's embarrassed. Maybe he's waiting for me to call him. I won't. He'll have to make the first move, and even then I don't know. I think that I would like to see him once more to ask some questions and to clear things up.

I'm heading north on Lake Shore Drive, near the spot where we discovered Howard Pore's body. I pull off and park the car facing the beach, watching a mean drizzle feed a turbulent lake. I'm about to turn off the engine when the newscaster mentions the name Andrew Malcolm. I turn the radio up: "...The governor is now approaching the podium. Joan Tatle of the United States Department of Justice and Assistant State's Attorney Lenore Weurster are also on the podium with Andrew Malcolm. Here's the governor now."

"Ladies and gentlemen of the media, thank you for coming here on such short notice. Two hours ago, Attorney General Byron advised me that he is resigning from his office, effective immediately. I have also been informed that Robert Hamilton, a chief aide of Attorney General Byron's, has also tendered his resignation. Although I am not privy to the exact nature of the information, I am told that there were certain improprieties in the office, which were uncovered by Ms. Tatle and Ms. Weurster in conjunction with Chief Jack Ryan of the Attorney General's Office.

"Apparently the Attorney General's office was protecting one of its informants from the consequences of a child abuse charge. The intentions of the Attorney General in so doing were above reproach. Informants are necessary to ferret out evil people who sell drugs to children. But as a result, a child may have died. The perpetrator of that horrendous act was recently murdered by his paramour, who then killed herself.

"Attorney General Byron has taken it upon himself to accept the blame for these actions and is retiring from the office, effective immediately. Also, I wish to add that two DCFS social workers also involved in this mishap have been transferred out of the Community Bound program. They have been reassigned to the child investigative unit and will receive additional training in the proper ways to preserve families.

"That's the bad news. Now for the good news: I am happy to report that we were able to prevail upon one of the leading attorneys, not just in the State of Illinois, but in the United States, to accept the job of Attorney General. Andrew Malcolm has generously agreed to give up his practice and take up this difficult challenge. Andrew, would you please say a few words?"

"Mr. Governor, ladies and gentlemen of the media, I am deeply moved at being offered this opportunity to use whatever talents God gave me to work with you and the people of this state. I conferred with my wife, Jennifer, who stands here next to me, before agreeing to accept this gracious offer, given the fact that our family's income will drop dramatically. But, as Jennifer put it, it's time to give back to the community. We—Jennifer, my children and I—eagerly and humbly accept this opportunity to serve the people of this great state.

"I'm new in the business of being in the public eye. I may not be the best Attorney General that Illinois has ever had, but I assure you that I will be the hardest-working. And I want you, the members of the working media, to hold me to that promise. I expect you to examine every aspect of my office and tell me and the people what we are doing wrong. Thank you very much—and now it's time to get to work."

I get out of the car, forgetting to put my rain slick on, and walk across the sand to the place where Howard's body was discovered and where now angry waves lash out and pound the shoreline. I think of Howard, Brenda, Jeanette, and wonder if Asha will escape their histories. And of Lilly and Sam: two losers, but one of whom may have found redemption. I smile as I recall the good people: Welch, Greenspan, Tate and Malone.

Suddenly I realize that I'm drenched and cold. I turn and walk back to the car wondering about Weurster, Tatle and Ryan: their futures, their morals, their compromises.

And what of Andrew? The man I loved, or thought I loved; and one for whom I almost compromised my family. Was I just a potential conquest? Somebody he wanted to fuck? Which ultimately he did.

And Jeffrey? Will I ever feel for him the passion I did for Andrew? Will I live out my youth and middle age sacrificing physical intimacy for the sake of two beautiful children? Will I have the courage to scuttle my relationship with Jeffrey? Or do I have the stomach, heart, soul, to try to make it all work?

I phone Jeff. "Can you get me the law school application?"

"Now you're talking. I'll have the papers tonight."

"What are you doing?"

"Staring out the window at the rain."

"How'd you like to meet me in 20 minutes?"

"Where?"

"Home."

"Huh?"

"Home."

"Why?"

"To make love. Wild, passionate, uninhibited love."

I wait for the "You're kidding," or "How about tonight?" Instead I get: "Twenty minutes."